Megan was ~~long, lean bod~~
the kitchen. H
with broad shoulders, and when he
rolled back the sleeves of his shirt
she saw that his arms were a faint
shade of golden brown. He was
irresistibly male—a man who would
melt any woman's heart.

Unnerved by his strong masculine presence, she sought something to do, filling the kettle with water and waiting for it to heat up.

In that moment he turned, so that his body was in intimate, immediate contact with hers, and she felt a wild flush of response reverberate throughout her nervous system. Every cell in her body tingled, clamouring for more. She loved the intimacy of that embrace, yet deep down she was afraid of what the consequences might be if she gave in to her wilder feelings and snuggled up against him as the arms wrapped around her were coaxing her to do. It had been a long, long day, and somehow her whole world seemed to have changed. Was it possible that she was falling for Theo? How else could she account for this tide of feeling that was sweeping over her?

When **Joanna Neil** discovered Mills & Boon®, her lifelong addiction to reading crystallised into an exciting new career writing Medical™ Romance. Her characters are probably the outcome of her varied lifestyle, which includes working as a clerk, typist, nurse and infant teacher. She enjoys dressmaking and cooking at her Leicestershire home. Her family includes a husband, son and daughter, an exuberant yellow Labrador and two slightly crazed cockatiels. She currently works with a team of tutors at her local education centre to provide creative writing workshops for people interested in exploring their own writing ambitions.

Recent titles by the same author:

CHILDREN'S DOCTOR, SOCIETY BRIDE
HIS VERY SPECIAL BRIDE
PROPOSING TO THE CHILDREN'S DOCTOR
A CONSULTANT BEYOND COMPARE
THE DOCTOR'S LONGED-FOR FAMILY

THE SURGEON SHE'S BEEN WAITING FOR

BY
JOANNA NEIL

MILLS & BOON®
Pure reading pleasure™

First published in Great Britain 2009
Harlequin Mills & Boon Limited,
Eton House, 18-24 Paradise Road, Richmond, Surrey TW9 1SR

© Joanna Neil 2009

ISBN: 978 0 263 86841 8

Set in Times Roman 10½ on 12¾ pt
03-0509-55633

Printed and bound in Spain
by Litografia Rosés, S.A., Barcelona

THE SURGEON SHE'S BEEN WAITING FOR

CHAPTER ONE

'How long are you going to be staying here?'

The sound of a child's voice cut through the gentle bird-song that filled the air, infiltrating the peace and quiet of the Welsh countryside.

Megan frowned. There was no one in sight, and she stopped for a moment, looking around to see if she could pinpoint exactly where the voice was coming from.

She had only just left the waterside inn behind, and now she was venturing into a neighbouring field, taking a well-worn footpath. The voice seemed to have originated from somewhere beyond the hedgerow that veiled the pub grounds from the disappearing line of the canal. In fact, the sound appeared to be coming from the direction in which she was heading right at this moment.

Most of the inn's customers were congregated happily around the wooden bench tables some distance away, enjoying the warm sunshine of a late May afternoon as they watched the canal boats drift by on their way towards the lock gates.

She heard a murmured reply. It was a man's voice, but she couldn't make out what he was saying. Somehow she hadn't expected that anyone would be stopping by this more secluded part of the canal, and for a moment the realisation made her pause. It was beginning to look as though her plan to take a quiet, solitary walk had been scuppered from the outset.

Not that it mattered. She had enjoyed a light meal and a companionable drink with her friend, Sarah, which had at least given her the chance to wind down a little after a difficult shift at the hospital. It had been a hectic few hours, and she was glad of the chance to loosen up a little. Even now, she could feel the pull of tight muscles in her neck and arms.

Now that Sarah had gone to meet up with her parents for a Sunday afternoon visit, Megan was free to wander as she pleased.

'Is you going to paint the swans?' The piping voice came again. 'I like them, but I like the ducks better.'

Again there was the muffled sound of a male voice answering, and this time it was closer. Megan followed the footpath through a gap in the hedgerow until she came upon the grassy canal bank once more.

A whole new vista appeared in front of her, and she took a moment to drink it in. A stone-built bridge spanned the water, and beyond that the canal opened up into a wide waterway, with fields on either side where sheep grazed. Further on, a breathtaking panorama of rolling hills and woodland spread out as far as the eye could see.

Nearby, a man was seated in front of an easel, a few feet away from the water's edge. He was wearing an open-necked, short-sleeved shirt and casual trousers, and from the taut, lean outline of his frame and the smooth, lightly bronzed appearance of his skin, she guessed he was in his early thirties. His dark hair was cut close to his head, in a style that complemented his angular features.

'Is that the sky?' A little boy, with the same, dark-coloured hair, waved his hand towards the canvas that the man was working on. He looked to be about four years old.

'Yes, it is.' The man's voice was deep and pleasant, easy on the ear.

The child looked up, turning his gaze heavenwards. 'The sky's blue. Why is the sky blue?'

'Because the light from the sun makes us see it that way.'

'Does it? Why?' The boy was puzzled.

The man dipped his brush into the palette of colours and added a fleck of white to his painting of the scene. 'Because the world is made up of colour.'

'Why?'

'Just because that's the way it is.'

Perhaps the boy sensed that he wasn't going to get any more answers to his questions, because he began to wander away from the man and his painting. He went over to the water's edge and peered down.

Megan guessed that he was looking at his reflection. He started to move his head from side to side, and then lifted up his arms and waggled his fingers. He began to giggle.

'My arms is wriggling,' the boy said. 'See? My face is wriggling as well.'

Megan felt herself tensing. The boy was far too close to the edge, and the man wasn't taking any notice of him at all. His concentration was centred on his painting.

'Are they?' he said. He wiped his brush on a cloth and glanced down at a box that rested by his feet.

'Why is they wriggling?'

The man glanced at the child briefly. 'I expect the water is moving,' he answered.

At least he had taken a moment to look at the boy, but his attention was short-lived. He rummaged in the wicker box and picked out a tube of paint, squeezing out a small amount onto his palette.

Megan stiffened. Her muscles were tightening up into knots all over again. Did the man not realise that the boy was dangerously close to the edge of the water? What would it take for him to notice that the ground was uneven, and one false move would tip the child into the river?

She walked towards the pair, and that was enough to prompt the man to glance in her direction. She ignored him. The boy was playing a jumping game, springing from one tuft of grass to another. At one point he seemed to stumble, but at the last moment he managed to steady himself, tilting his arms sideways like the wings of an aeroplane.

'I think you should come away from the water's edge,' Megan said softly, moving to intercept the boy as he teetered on the brink once more. 'The ground is very uneven just here, and you could slip.'

The child frowned, his gaze moving out over the water. 'Is it very deep?'

'It's hard to say,' Megan told him, 'but it could be. I shouldn't like you to fall in.'

The boy nodded, and moved to a safe distance. He began to pick up pebbles from the footpath and started to throw them into the water one by one.

Satisfied that the child was out of immediate danger, Megan directed her gaze towards the man. He was adding a hint of gold-green to his painting, highlighting the way the sunlight filtered through the reeds on the riverbank.

'That's a beautiful painting,' she murmured, going to look at the canvas, and it was the truth. He had captured the image of the countryside in glorious, perfect detail, and he obviously had a definite talent for the art. At any other time she would have liked to talk to him about his skills, but right now there were other, more pressing things on her mind. 'I wonder, though, whether you ought to be paying attention to something other than the scenery at the moment?'

He sent her a brief, unconcerned glance, before returning his gaze to his canvas. 'And that would be…?'

Megan's jaw tightened. 'Has it not occurred to you that this child is too young to be roaming unsupervised so near the canal?'

His glance went fleetingly to the boy. 'He seems to be reasonably surefooted.'

She lifted a brow and shook her head in despair at his answer. 'I'm not certain that reasonably surefooted is quite good enough. He's too close to the water's edge.'

He looked along the canal bank, a small line indenting his brow. 'Do you think so? Perhaps you're worrying unnecessarily. I doubt children are quite as reckless as you might imagine.'

Megan pulled in a sharp breath, simmering flame sparking in her grey eyes. 'Is that all you have to say? How would you react if he were to fall in? I dare say your painting would have to take second place then—or perhaps I'm wrong in assuming that?'

He turned to look at her, his gaze shifting over her more intently this time, moving slowly downwards to follow the curving line of her snugly fitting cotton top and sweeping over the blue jeans that faithfully moulded her hips. Her whole body stiffened as he brought his glance back to her face. A flush of warmth flowed along her cheekbones.

'You might have a point there,' he intoned drily. 'I expect in that case I would have to go and fish him out, and then we would both end up soaked to the skin.'

Megan threw him an exasperated look. 'Is that it? Is that as much as you care?'

His blue eyes darkened a fraction, taking on a smoke grey tinge. 'You seem to be expecting something from me,' he murmured. 'Do you think perhaps you're being a little uptight about this?'

Megan tossed back her head, sending the chestnut sweep of her hair into tumbling chaos as it fell across her shoulders. 'Uptight?' she echoed. 'You think I'm uptight?' She bit the words out through her teeth. 'The boy could have drowned. Don't you have any protective instincts whatsoever? I just don't understand how parents can care so little about what their children get up to. Doesn't it bother you at all that he might have slipped?'

He nodded. 'Well, yes, of course, that would have been unfortunate, and it would have been even more disturbing if I'd had to go in after him. Actually, though, what concerns me most is that he's here at all.'

'I don't think I follow what you're saying.'

'I don't suppose you do.' He frowned. 'The fact is he isn't my child. To begin with, I thought he was with you, but that's obviously not the case.' His mouth made a wry shape. 'Unfortunately, it also means that I'm going to have to find out who he does belong to if a parent doesn't come along soon.'

Megan was dumbfounded. She had been convinced that the boy belonged with him, and now she was rapidly searching for some way to make up for the way she had spoken to him. What must he be thinking? A total stranger barged in on him and invaded his privacy, accusing him of all sorts of things. It was unforgivable.

'I'm sorry,' she said awkwardly. 'I thought, because you were together out here, that he was your son. Clearly, that was a mistake.'

'Yes, I can see how you might have formed that impression, but even so I wonder if perhaps your instincts are a bit too highly charged. Maybe you should try to relax a little more.'

Relax? He was the expert in doing that, wasn't he? If he were any more laid-back he would topple over. No matter who the child belonged to, he might have been a tad more cautious in watching out for him. She bent her head momentarily and silently ground her teeth together.

'Whatever,' she said after a second or two, straightening up once more. 'There's still the problem of the child.' She thought things through for a moment. 'I wonder if he's wandered over here from the pub? Surely someone must be missing him?'

He shrugged. 'As you said, some people don't seem to care what their children get up to—but maybe there's some other explanation.'

Just then a young girl came hurrying along the footpath. 'Nicky,' she was calling. 'Nicky, where are you?'

'Ah,' the man said under his breath. 'Perhaps here is our answer. I felt sure it would all come right if we waited long enough.' His glance went to the boy, who had stopped throwing pebbles into the water and was turning around to look at the girl. 'I wonder if this is young Nicky?'

Surely the girl was too young to be his mother? Megan studied her. She must only be around fifteen years old. Maybe she was his sister.

'Nicky,' the girl said in a cross voice, 'what are you doing here? I've been looking everywhere for you. You know you shouldn't wander off. Your mum is worried about you.'

'Is she?' Nicky asked, with the innocence of childhood. 'Why is she worried?'

The girl gave an exasperated sigh. 'Your dad is poorly. Your mother has better things to do than chase after you. You had better come with me.'

'My dad's not poorly,' Nicky said with a frown. 'He's having a picnic.'

'Well, he's poorly now, and your mum has enough to think about without worrying about where you are.' The girl took hold of Nicky's hand, and turned to look at Megan. 'I don't suppose you have a phone that we could use, do you? My auntie's panicking a bit. She tried to call for an ambulance, but the battery's gone on her phone.'

'Actually, I'm a doctor,' Megan said, immediately alert. 'Maybe I could help in some way. Do you want me to come and see what's wrong? Is it your uncle who's ill?'

'Yes, it is. It would be great if you wouldn't mind coming along to help us.' The girl sounded relieved. 'We thought he was choking, because he couldn't get his words out properly, and then my aunt thought he'd had a stroke, because his mouth went all strange. She didn't know what to do.'

Megan felt sure that if the man's condition was bad enough to stop the woman coming to find her child, it was probably important enough to merit attention. She was already starting to walk back along the footpath the way she had come.

She sent a swift look in the artist's direction, wondering whether he might decide to come and help out, but he wasn't moving. His expression was watchful and at the same time guarded, an odd kind of what might be world-weariness shadowing his features. He was probably ruing the way his tranquil afternoon had been disturbed, but Megan couldn't find it in her to care either way. His attitude still annoyed her.

Nicky skipped along beside his cousin, unconcerned by all the palaver, and she was glad that at least one little mystery had been cleared up.

In a meadow nearby the child's father was lying on the grass in the shade of the hedgerow. His distressed wife was loosening his shirt around the collar, but she looked up as Megan and the girl approached.

'Oh, thank goodness…you found him, Chloe,' she said, sending the girl a relieved look. 'I was so distracted. I just didn't see him wander off.'

She broke off, obviously too concerned about her husband to say any more on that score.

'He hadn't gone far, Auntie Alice.'

The woman swallowed hard. 'Thanks for bringing him back. Will you keep an eye on him for me?' Chloe nodded, and Alice turned back to her husband. 'William,' she said in agitation, 'you have to tell me what's wrong. Is it the lager that you were drinking? Did it go down the wrong way? Has it upset your stomach? You need to try to tell me what's happening. It can't be the food—you haven't eaten anything.'

William mumbled something incoherent, and Megan knelt down beside him. 'Chloe told me your husband wasn't feeling well,' she told Alice. 'I'm a doctor. Is it all right if I take a look at him?'

Alice gave a relieved gulp. 'Would you? Oh, please do. I'd be so glad if you could do anything to help. He keeps writhing about, as if he's in pain. He hasn't been well for a while before this, but we thought it was just general aches and pains. We were hoping that an afternoon out would help to make him feel better. I've never seen him like this before.'

'OK.' Megan looked to see if William was responsive. 'Hello, William. I'm Dr Rees,' she told him, and his mouth moved but no sound came out. She set about checking his pulse. 'His heart rate is very rapid,' she said, looking up at Alice. 'I really need to go and get my medical bag. It's in my car, back at the pub, along with my phone. It won't take me more than a few minutes.'

As she started to move away, she saw that the man from the canal bank had ventured over, presumably to see what was going on.

'He doesn't look too good, does he?' he said, shooting a glance over to where Nicky's father was lying. 'I'll call for an ambulance.'

'Thanks,' she murmured. 'That would be a great help.' A glance showed her that he had left his painting materials behind, and that seemed incongruous to her. The boy's flirtation with danger had not been enough to make him leave his painting, but the notion that an adult was in difficulty had clearly caught his attention.

Or perhaps he was right, and she was the one who had things the wrong way about. Maybe she was too tense for her own good. Either way, his comments still rankled and, whatever the reality of the situation, she quickly dismissed him from her mind.

She was back at William's side just a short time later.

'I'm going to give him oxygen,' she told Alice. 'It should help him to breathe a little more easily, but I need you to assist me, if you would.' She worked quickly, placing the breathing mask over William's nose and mouth and securing it in place. 'Do you think you could hold this oxygen bag and keep squeezing it for me like this?'

'Yes, I can do that.'

'Good.' Megan began to wrap a blood-pressure cuff around William's arm.

'What's the matter with my daddy?'

Megan looked up to see that Nicky was anxiously watching what was happening.

'He's not feeling very well, Nicky,' she said. 'We need to send him to hospital so that the doctors can make him more comfortable.'

Nicky stuck his thumb in his mouth, his eyes wide and troubled. Megan looked up at Chloe. 'I wonder if you could take him to look at the ducks?' she suggested softly. 'This is perhaps a little too upsetting for him.'

The girl nodded, and Megan tacked on, 'Just keep an eye on him and see to it that he doesn't go too close to the water.'

'I will.' Chloe took off with Nicky in the direction of the canal wharf. 'Come on, squirt,' she said. 'We'll see how many ducklings we can find.'

'Do you have any idea what might be wrong with my husband?' the woman asked.

'Not yet,' Megan answered. 'They'll have to do tests at the hospital, and possibly a scan.' She was concerned about the way his muscles were twitching, and as she watched him his body began to jerk uncontrollably. 'Does he have any history of epilepsy?'

The woman shook her head. 'No. The only thing he ever mentioned is a sort of cramping pain from time to time.'

'Show me where it was that he had the pain,' Megan said, and the man's wife showed her an area around his kidneys.

'Is that any help to you?' the woman asked.

'Possibly, but we won't know anything for sure until he's undergone thorough tests.' Megan frowned. 'His blood pressure is very high. Has he had problems with that before?'

'Not that I am aware of, although he has been getting head-aches. Is it important?'

'It could be. I'm going to have to give him an injection to control the seizures,' Megan murmured. 'With any luck, the ambulance will be here before too long.'

The paramedics arrived within a few minutes, and Megan supervised William's transfer into the ambulance, walking with them to the pub car park, where their vehicle was waiting.

'I thought your stint on duty had finished a few hours ago,' the lead paramedic said, acknowledging Megan. He grinned. 'You can't stay away, that's the truth of it, isn't it?'

'Too right,' she said with a faint smile. 'I expect I'll see you again bright and early tomorrow.'

'I want to go with my husband,' Alice put in. 'Can I do that, and take Chloe and Nicky with me?'

The driver nodded. 'We should be able to squeeze you in.' He ushered them inside the vehicle and then closed the doors on them, leaving his partner to attend to the patient on the journey. 'We'll be on our way, then,' he told Megan.

She inclined her head and waved them off. Then she turned, and realised that the artist was standing just a short distance away, watching her.

'You seem to know them quite well,' he said, throwing a glance towards the disappearing ambulance. 'Are they colleagues of yours?'

'Yes, I see them most days. I work in the A and E department at the Borderlands Hospital.'

'Ah.' He tilted his head backwards a fraction, and for a moment she wondered if there was something familiar about him.

'Have we met before this?' she asked him on an impulse. 'I suddenly have the feeling that I've seen you around and about.'

He smiled briefly. 'It's possible, I suppose, though I doubt it. I'm sure I would have remembered if we'd been introduced.' His glance shimmered over her. He put out his hand and she lifted hers in return, feeling more than a little overwhelmed as his palm covered hers in a warm embrace. 'I'm Theo Benyon,' he said, drawing her close to him.

'Megan Rees.'

'Perhaps we'll meet again before too long?' he murmured. His blue gaze drifted over her.

'It's possible, I dare say.' She sent him a long look from under thick, dark lashes, an imp of mischief coming to her. 'If you're not too busy with your painting, you might want to help out in one of my "Keep Children Safe" workshops. We run them from time to time at the hospital, and we're always looking for people to lend a hand.'

He threw back his head and laughed. 'You don't give up, do you, Megan Rees? I guess you like to involve people in your good causes—but I think I'll pass on that one if it's all the same with you. I have quite enough to deal with at the moment, one way and another.'

'Do you?' She wondered what those things might be as she smiled gently and tugged her hand free. 'I have to go,' she said. 'Things to do, people to see. I'll leave you to go and retrieve your painting.'

It was an excuse, but suddenly she felt the need to put distance between them. Her hand was still tingling from the warm intimacy of his grasp and her body quivered in response to the lingering look he had bestowed on her. All at once he seemed like the Devil personified, and her instinct was to retreat, fast.

She wasn't quite sure why she felt that way, but if instinct was urging her to run, she would follow it. Theo was a red-blooded male, young and vigorous, and she couldn't help but sense his interest in her. That alone was enough to put her on her guard. Hadn't she already discovered that there was some kind of a flaw in all the men who crossed her path?

CHAPTER TWO

'IT WAS definitely a heart attack. Look at the lab results...they show that her cardiac enzymes are elevated.' Megan scanned the report on screen and then switched to the results of the echocardiograph. 'See this area here?' She glanced at the senior house officer by her side and pointed out the region that was giving her concern. 'The heart function is definitely impaired.'

'I see it. It's not good, is it?' Sarah winced. Her face was pale against the gold of her hair, and Megan guessed the long hours on duty were beginning to take their toll on her. She hoped she could send her to the doctors' lounge to take a well-earned rest soon, as things had been hectic in A and E.

'Not good at all.' Megan turned her attention to the monitor that was recording her patient's vital signs. 'Her heart rate is way too high and her condition's deteriorating fast.'

'What are you going to do?' Sarah was worried, her gaze troubled as she studied the laboratory results. 'You've already given her glyceryl trinitrate and diamorphine, along with an infusion of tirofiban and heparin, but the chest pain is coming back, and she's struggling to get her breath.'

Megan pressed her lips together. 'We'll leave her on the infusion for a while longer to see if things settle down.' She frowned, pushing back a silky lock of chestnut hair that tumbled across her cheek. 'Is there any news of Mr Carlson yet? We're running out of time. If we don't get her to surgery soon, she could go into cardiogenic shock and that would be grim.'

'I'll go and check, but last I heard he was tied up in Theatre at a hospital across the county.'

Megan winced. 'We really need more people that we can call on. We've been understaffed for months now, and the situation doesn't show any sign of changing for the better, does it?'

Sarah shook her head. She went to make her phone call, while Megan spoke quietly to the nurse who was assisting, before checking the infusion meter and keying in the appropriate settings.

'Let me know if there's any change,' she murmured, and the nurse nodded.

'I will.'

Megan drew in a quick breath and went in search of her next patient. It had been non-stop from the minute she had come on duty. A traffic accident at a notorious road junction had kept her and her colleagues busy for most of the morning, tending to the injured, and then she'd had to deal with a patient who couldn't breathe properly and a child with a broken arm. Then had come the woman who had suffered a heart attack.

Just another day in the emergency department, and problems were piling up on one another, thick and fast. Wasn't that the nature of the job?

An hour or so later she headed towards the central area to see who was next on her list.

'Ouch.' A small voice caught her attention and she glanced into one of the treatment rooms off the central area in time to see a small boy clambering up onto a trolley bed. He was attempting to unhook an oxygen mask and tubing from the outlet on the wall at the back of the bed, and it looked as though he had banged his leg in the attempt. He stopped to rub his injury momentarily and then went on with his examination of the oxygen equipment.

What on earth was he doing in there on his own? Megan went to investigate.

'Is someone looking after you?' she asked. He couldn't be much more than five years old, she guessed.

The boy glanced at her and then nodded without saying anything.

'Are you sick?'

He shook his head.

'That's good. But I saw that you banged your leg on the bed. Do you want me to take a look at it?'

Again there was a perfunctory shake of the head, an action that sent his dark hair into a quiver. Losing interest in her, he tugged at the tubing and started to play around with the mask.

'You really shouldn't be playing with that,' she told him. 'If you pull on it like that it might get damaged, and then it won't be of any use if we need it when someone needs help to breathe.'

'Oh.' He put the mask down on the pillow and looked around him in a disgruntled fashion. 'I don't want to stay here,' he said, giving her an accusatory glance. 'I want my mum.'

'OK.' Megan studied him, wondering what had brought about the downward slant to his lip. 'I'll see if we can do something about that.' She held out her hand to him. 'Do you want to come with me and we'll see if we can sort this out?'

His glare was truculent. 'I don't know you. You're a stranger.'

'Ah…' For a second or two his simple logic knocked her for six. 'Well, yes, you're quite right about that,' she murmured, recovering. 'And it's very sensible of you to stay put, under the circumstances.' Her mouth twisted as she thought things through. 'Who is supposed to be looking after you?' she asked, trying another tack. 'You really shouldn't be here on your own, you know.'

A boy of few words, he pointed to the central area beyond, and then shrugged his shoulders upwards, clamping his bent legs with his arms and burying his chin on his knees. Watching him, Megan didn't think she was going to get much more out of him.

She looked to where he had pointed and saw that Sarah was talking to someone who had his back to her. She stared for a moment at that tall, grey-suited figure, and all at once she stiffened. There was something instantly recognisable about those broad masculine shoulders and the long sweep of taut legs.

What was Theo Benyon doing here? And did he make a habit of leaving children to their own devices?

'Stay here,' Megan said to the child. 'What's your name, by the way? What should I call you?'

'Harry.' His blue eyes held a belligerent spark, but she sensed that underneath all the muted aggression there was a troubled, vulnerable little boy.

'I'll be back in a little while, Harry.'

Sarah was clearly captivated by the artist's easygoing manner. There was a flush of warmth in her once pale cheeks, and her green eyes were lit with a kind of awed expectation.

Megan clamped her lips together. Theo was a disruptive influence. Why was he taking up space in their A and E unit if he wasn't sick?

'Well, hello, there,' she said on a brisk note as she approached him. 'I wasn't expecting to see you again quite so soon. Is there something we can do for you, Mr Benyon?'

'Theo, please.' A faint smile hovered on his lips, but it disappeared almost as soon as he met her gaze. 'Uh-oh,' he said, narrowing his eyes. 'Am I in trouble again? I seem to recognise that expression on your face. It's the look that says, You had better watch your step, because I'm not best pleased.'

'I can't imagine why you should think that way,' she murmured. Turning to Sarah, she said softly, 'Why don't you go and take a break for a while, Sarah? Things seem to be calm around here for the moment.'

Sarah smiled. 'You know that's the cue for all hell to break loose, don't you?'

Megan's mouth curved briefly. 'I do, but we'll manage somehow if it does.'

'Good. I could do with a coffee. I'll just check on my patients, though, before I go.' Sarah glanced at Theo. 'It was interesting talking to you. I'm sorry I couldn't be of any help.'

She walked away, leaving Megan to direct her attention towards Theo. 'I hardly like to bring the subject up,' Megan said in an even tone, 'but young Harry over there says he belongs with you and he doesn't look to be a very happy bunny right now. I'm afraid he might get into mischief if he's left to his own devices for much longer.'

Theo frowned, as though he had no idea what she was talking about. 'I've just rescued the oxygen equipment from his inquisitive fingers,' she explained, 'and...' her glance went to the treatment room, a line indenting her brow '...it looks as though he's moved on from there. It would be my guess that the trolley bed is about to go walkabout any moment now.'

Theo's blue eyes narrowed. 'He was supposed to be looking at picture books.'

Her mouth flattened. 'Was he? I can't imagine why he's not looking at them when there's a whole ward full of gadgets to explore.' Her tone held a hint of sarcasm. 'Clever boy. It can't have taken him above two seconds to figure out the

wheel-release mechanism.' Her brows met in a fine, dark line.
'I just hope he's worked out how the brake operates.'

'I don't know about clever,' Theo said under his breath. 'What
Harry has in abundance is determination. Excuse me.' He was
already striding purposefully towards the treatment room.

A moment later he was back again, with a scowling Harry
in tow. 'I want to see my mum,' the boy said.

'You will.' Theo lightly tousled the boy's hair. 'Just let me
apologise to the doctor for leaving you to fend for yourself.
She thinks I don't know how to look after young children, and
you've more or less proved her point.' He turned his gaze on
Megan once more, treating her to the full blaze of eyes that
were the colour of a summer sky.

'I was entirely in the wrong,' he said, bowing his head in
a way that might have signified contrition, if she hadn't caught
the faint glimmer of a smile in that devilish glance. 'I thought
I could rely on him to stay out of trouble for a minute or two
while I left a message for Mr Edwards, but obviously my faith
was misplaced.'

'I dare say these things happen,' she returned evenly, 'though
I don't know of any child who can resist exploring. But I guess
things turned out all right in the end. It would probably be better
if you were to keep him by your side from now on.'

'I'll do that.' His mouth pulled wrily. 'I'll take him away
and we'll leave you in peace.'

Megan nodded. She might have said more, but he was
already starting to turn away from her, and the nurse who had
been assisting with the cardiac patient came hurrying forward,
saying in an anxious tone, 'Mrs Claremont is going downhill
fast. I think she's going into cardiogenic shock—all the signs
you said to look out for are there, and her circulation appears
to be shutting down. Will you come?'

'Of course. Phone through to the catheter suite and tell them I need to operate, will you, and ask the senior house officer on duty to assist me? I'll need two nurses to come along as well.' She started to swivel around in order to hurry back to the observation ward, but added, 'I don't suppose there has been any news from Mr Carlson?'

'He phoned to say it'll be several hours before he can get away. He said to put her on thrombolytics.'

Megan winced. 'We've done that, but it isn't working. I've no choice but to do an emergency angiography and try to open up the blood vessel with a balloon implant. I just hope we can buy her some time.'

She glanced back towards Theo, something in her drawn to seek him out. He, too, had stopped in his tracks, she discovered, and he was watching her, an odd expression on his face, one that she could not read, no matter how she tried. Then Harry tugged on his arm and he gathered himself together and reluctantly began to turn in the direction of the exit.

Megan continued on her way. Perhaps it was just as well that he had gone. Somehow he was managing to cloud her vision and cause a blip in her usually clear thinking. 'You had better let Mr Edwards know what we're doing,' she said to the nurse. 'He wanted to be kept informed.'

'OK. I'll page him. He was working with a patient in Resus a while ago.'

Megan hurried to check on her patient. The woman's renal system was failing despite the intravenous diuretics and medications she had received.

'Let's get her up to the catheter suite,' she said, when the nurse returned. 'I'm guessing that she has a critically narrowed artery, and I need to restore her circulation as soon as possible.'

The hour that followed was nerve-racking. Megan introduced a catheter into an artery in her patient's groin and guided it into the descending aorta, the heart's main blood vessel, monitoring her progress all the time with the aid of the computer. 'OK, I see the blockage and I have the balloon in place. We need to set up the pump so that it will inflate and deflate the balloon at the right intervals.'

They worked as a team, and then watched the pump in action to ensure that it was working properly. When the patient's heart was in the resting phase, the balloon inflated, increasing the supply of oxygen-rich blood to the coronary arteries. When the heart was ready to work, the balloon deflated, decreasing the workload on the heart.

'Well done, everybody,' Megan said, moving away from the bedside some time later. 'We've done all we can for now, and we've managed to restore her circulation for the time being. The balloon can stay in place until Mr Carlson is ready to operate.'

Her boss, Mr Edwards, met up with her as she was leaving the catheter suite. 'How did it go?' he asked.

'She's stable for the time being.' Megan's expression was troubled. 'I just hope Mr Carlson will be able to do a coronary bypass before too long. She's in desperate need of the surgery. She's still relatively young, and she has a family waiting for her.'

'It's always a worrying time for all concerned.' Mr Edwards walked with her to the lift. He was a tall man, distinguished-looking, with steel-grey hair that was cut close to frame his head. 'By the way, the nurse on Reception told me Theo Benyon was in here looking for me. She said she saw you talking to him, but then he left... Was there a problem? Do you happen to know where he went?'

Did her boss know the man? Megan shook her head. 'I've

no idea. I was just relieved that he gathered up the child that was with him and kept him from getting into any more mischief. I was worried that the equipment would be damaged if he didn't rein him in.'

Mr Edwards frowned. 'You didn't say anything to annoy him, did you?'

'No. At least, I don't think so. I may have been a trifle curt with him, I suppose.' She sent him an enquiring look. 'Why…is there a problem? Is it to do with the artwork you were thinking of commissioning?' It suddenly occurred to her that Theo was an artist, and Mr Edwards had been talking about having the children's wing of A and E spruced up—was Theo famous for his murals, or something? 'Is that why he was here, to see you about artwork for the children's unit?'

'Artwork? No, not at all. Nothing like that.' Mr Edwards was unusually distracted as he pressed the button for the lift. 'I operated on the boy's mother—I expect he wanted to talk to me about that. I hope you didn't say or do anything to upset him?'

Megan sent him a confused glance. It wasn't like her boss to be so edgy and preoccupied. Had something gone wrong during the operation? That would be a tragedy in itself, but it was unlikely to have been Mr Edwards's fault. He was an excellent surgeon with an impressive track record.

It was all very puzzling. What was wrong with the boy's mother? And if his wife was seriously ill, what had Theo been thinking of when he'd lightly flirted with her? Or had she misjudged his actions? It was possible, of course, or perhaps he was one of those men who saw every woman as a challenge. Either way, the man had a lot to answer for.

'As I was saying,' she said as they stepped into the lift, 'I spoke to Mr Benyon, but I simply suggested that the boy needed to be taken in hand. Of course, I didn't realise that the child's mother was ill. No wonder Harry was acting up. He must be very worried about her.'

'Yes, I expect he is. Anyway, if you run into Theo again, go carefully. I don't want to alienate him in any way.'

And what was that supposed to mean? She opened her mouth to ask him, but her boss was frowning heavily, deep in thought and locked away in some world of his own. It wasn't at all like him to be this way, and Megan had no idea what to make of it. Perhaps, though, this was not the best time to start quizzing him.

Anyway, with any luck she wouldn't run into Theo again any time soon.

The lift came to a halt and they stepped out into the corridor. Mr Edwards headed straight towards his office, and Megan decided to go in search of a late lunch.

Sarah was just preparing to leave her table at the cafeteria when Megan set down her lunch-tray.

'I heard you had to operate,' Sarah said. 'Do you think Mrs Claremont will pull through OK?'

'I hope so. It all depends on whether Mr Carlson will be able to operate successfully. She's very weak.'

'That's hardly surprising, but you've done everything that you could for her.' Sarah glanced at Megan before pushing her chair back from the table and getting to her feet. Her green eyes were sympathetic. 'No one could have done anything more, and they'll take good care of her in the intensive care unit. It's just a question of waiting to see what happens.'

'I know.' Megan sighed and gazed back at her friend. 'Dealing with a heart attack is difficult enough at any time, but when it happens to a relatively young mother it's heartbreaking.'

Sarah nodded and glanced down at her watch. 'I have to

get back to work,' she said, tucking a strand of golden hair back into place. 'I'll see you later, Megan. Try to eat something. It will make you feel better and help to keep your strength up.'

'I will.' Megan toyed with the salad on her plate, twirling her fork idly in the mound of grated cheese, as she watched her friend walk away.

The food tasted good, and she ate carefully, savouring the variety of flavours—honey-baked ham, crisp red and green peppers and a crusty bread roll.

For just a few moments it was good to relax and enjoy the freedom from responsibility. This job meant everything to her, but she had to acknowledge that she was in real need of a break.

As difficult as it was, heart-rending though it might be at times, her career in medicine was her life. She had worked hard to come this far, and as a specialist registrar in A and E she had a good deal of responsibility resting on her shoulders...shoulders that ached right now with a growing knot of tension.

She put down her fork and sipped at her hot cup of coffee, moving her limbs to ease the tightness in her muscles. It was a relief to be able to unwind for a few precious minutes. Stretching her legs out in front of her, she let her mind drift over the variety of cases she'd had to deal with so far today.

It was as though every minute was taken up with life-and-death decisions, and she faced a struggle each day to keep one step ahead. Why did she put herself through all this?

She stared out of the window as though she might find the answer in the tubs of brightly coloured pansies that were dotted about the paved quadrangle.

'Hello, there... Meeting up like this is getting to be something of a habit.'

Megan gave a start and looked up as the sound of that familiar male voice intruded on her reverie.

'You're right. So it is.' She stared at Theo Benyon. What on earth was he doing there?

'Sorry, I didn't mean to startle you.' He was holding a tray, laden with a coffee cup and pastries, and now he asked, 'Would it be all right if I join you?'

'Help yourself.' She waved a hand towards the chair opposite.

He sat down, his gaze shooting over her as he stirred his coffee with a spoon. 'You look wiped out,' he murmured. 'Have things not been going too well for you?'

She sent him a wry smile. 'What was the give-away—the dark shadows under my eyes or my general drawn appearance?' He, of course, looked absolutely great. His grey suit was beautifully tailored, cut from dark fabric that looked fabulously expensive. His jacket was open, so that she could see the fine linen of his shirt, and his tie was subtly patterned to blend in with the whole.

His mouth made an odd quirk. 'Nothing like that. You just look generally weary.'

Her mouth flattened. 'It's been a difficult day, one way and another.'

He lifted a brow in query. 'Last I saw of you, you were headed up to the catheter suite. Did things not go too well?'

'They went well enough. My patient suffered a myocardial infarction—a heart attack—and unfortunately it took a long while for her to be brought into hospital in the first place. She lives out in a remote rural area. It never helps if the patient goes for a long time without receiving specialised attention. She was only in her early forties and eventually she went into cardiogenic shock. It was all we could do to bring her back from the brink.'

She pressed her lips together, and then glanced at his plate and the pastries. 'It looks as though you have a sweet tooth,' she murmured, changing the subject. 'Are you planning on eating all of those by yourself?'

'Not necessarily.' He sent her an amused look. 'You're welcome to choose one if you like. I recommend the fruit tart. Just save the jam doughnut for Harry. That's his favourite, and he'll be coming along to demolish it just as soon as he's finished with the vending machine. I think he's trying to nab himself a small rubber ball…not one of his best ideas, because you can bet it will bounce all over the place and be lost in no time at all.'

'Ah, I wondered what had happened to him.' She glanced across the room to the machine where the boy was gazing thoughtfully at a collection of coloured balls. 'Thanks all the same, but I'm content with my salad.'

She looked at him more closely. 'So is this where I've seen you before? Are you visiting a patient here?'

'I am. As you say, that's probably it. I've been here several times over the last couple of weeks.'

'It must be difficult for you, fitting in visits around work and taking time to look after Harry as well. Or perhaps you're able to work from home? I imagine that painting must be the ideal job.'

His mouth curved, lending a roguish slant to his features. 'I'm flattered you think I could make a decent living from it, but I haven't actually put it to the test. Anyway, I have Harry to look after just now, and that's a full-time job in itself.'

'Oh, I see. I mean… Yes, I can imagine that it is.'

Harry came over to the table, hefting a small rubber ball in his palm. 'I got it,' he said. 'I wanted the red one with the white swirls, and I got it. See?' He opened out his palm to show it to Theo.

'That's obviously a very special one,' Theo remarked. 'Just see that it doesn't roll about the floor and get in everybody's way.'

It was already too late as he spoke. Harry gleefully tried out the ball for bounce-ability, and what followed was an excited chase to retrieve it from under the nearby tables.

Theo's mouth set in a resigned expression. 'Hold onto it, or I'll look after it for you,' he warned.

Turning back to Megan, he said thoughtfully, 'I meant to ask how the man from the pub fared after his collapse. Did you manage to follow up on what happened to him?'

Megan nodded. 'I did. The doctor who looked after him on admission to hospital has ordered tests, including a CT scan. We'll know more in a day or so, but for the moment he's comfortable.'

'That's something, anyway.'

The rubber ball was on the loose once more, and as quick as a flash Theo caught it, enclosing it in his palm.

'I want to play with it,' Harry said. 'Can I have it back, please?'

Theo shook his head. 'Not until we get home. People in here are sick, or upset because they're visiting relatives who aren't well. They don't want to be having to duck out of the way of your ball every few seconds.'

Harry's lip jutted in a belligerent fashion. 'I'll keep hold of it, I promise.'

'No, you won't. I'll look after it until we get home.'

Harry opened his mouth to protest but thought better of it at the last moment. He turned his attention to Megan. 'Do you work here?' he asked.

She nodded. 'I do, and actually I should be getting back to work right now. I have patients to see.' She swallowed the last dregs of her coffee, and glanced across the table at Theo. 'I expect you have things you need to be doing, as well.'

'He said he would take me fishing,' Harry said, nodding vigorously. 'And we're going to plant things in the garden so it's nice for Mummy when she comes home, and then we're going shopping to get me some new clothes.'

'That sounds as though you have lots to look forward to,' Megan acknowledged with a faint smile. Did his father not do any kind of work? For all he denied it, it sounded as though he must make some money from his paintings. Perhaps he was simply being modest about his talent, or maybe he was a man of independent means. Then again, he could simply be taking a vacation in order to take care of his son. Why was she even questioning how he came to be there or how he lived his life? What was it about him that provoked her curiosity?

'I heard that you were looking for Mr Edwards,' she said, looking directly at Theo as she stood up. 'Last I saw of him, he was heading for his office. I gathered he would like to speak to you, too.'

Theo frowned, then nodded. 'I'll go and find him. Thank you for letting me know.'

'You're welcome.' She sent the boy a quick smile. ''Bye, Harry. I hope your mother feels better soon.'

'So do I,' he said. 'I don't like my mum being poorly. I want her to be back home with me.'

'Of course you do.' Megan gave him a sympathetic smile. Any child would want his mother to be with him, wouldn't he? Wasn't it the most natural thing in the world to wish for? And yet it was the one yearning she had struggled with throughout her own life, that even now she found difficulty coming to terms with. Why was it that she had never experienced that particular joy? Was she so unlovable that her own mother had not wanted to stay around to be with her through her childhood?

'Are you all right?' Theo asked gently.

She gave a small start, coming out of her introspection to glance briefly at him. 'Of course. I'm absolutely fine.'

Then she turned and hurried away quickly. She didn't want Theo's quiet concern. He stirred up all that had lain dormant inside her and her emotions were in turmoil, though for the life of her she couldn't have said why.

She needed to escape.

CHAPTER THREE

'YOU said that you would like to see William's results when they came back,' Mr Edwards said, holding a manila folder aloft and calling Megan over to his side. 'You remember the man you sent in to us who collapsed by the canal? I have the radiologist's report here, and you can see the films on the computer screen.'

Megan went over to the desk. 'What was the outcome? I guessed he might be low on magnesium, among other things, but that could have been caused by all manner of illnesses.'

'You were right. Take a look at the film and tell me what you see.'

She scanned the pictures on the screen and drew in a quick breath. 'It's a tumour, isn't it?' She pointed towards the image. 'There, on the adrenal gland. No wonder he's been having problems.' She glanced at her boss. 'What happens now? Will he go for surgery?'

John Edwards nodded. 'He's on the schedule for next week. Let's hope there are no complications.'

'At least he has a diagnosis. That's a positive start.'

'True.' He glanced at his watch. 'I have to go, or I shall be late for my meeting. I'll leave you to hold the fort while I'm away. If Theo Benyon should come in at any time over the next couple of hours, page me, will you?'

She frowned. 'Is he likely to do that?'

He nodded. 'I asked him if he had any landscape paintings that we could put up in the waiting room. He said he might have something for us to look at.'

'OK.' Megan absorbed that. 'So I should show him around, should I? Maybe point out where the paintings might go?'

'Yes, anything. Grab him, give him a coffee and, whatever you do, don't let him escape. He's proving to be quite elusive, but I really need to talk to him.'

Megan frowned. 'I thought you already did that?'

'Only for a couple of minutes. He seemed to be in a hurry to go somewhere, but I suspect it was just an excuse.'

Surely he had that wrong? Megan couldn't imagine why Theo would be trying to avoid spending any more time than necessary with her boss. 'I don't think I follow any of this. What's it all about? Did something go wrong with an operation? What's the big mystery?'

'No mystery. I just need to get him on our side. We need him here. He's the most skilled surgeon for miles around, he's here in our territory, and he's not working at the moment, so it's a great opportunity to get him to stay here at our hospital.'

Her jaw dropped for a second or two before she managed to get herself together again. 'He's a surgeon?' she echoed faintly. 'I thought he was here because he was visiting a patient. I thought he was an artist…'

John looked at her blankly. 'Yes, yes, that's all true…but I had the good fortune to operate on poor Francie, and he was pleased enough to come and thank me, so we have a fantastic opportunity, you see. We can't let him slip away.'

Megan shook her head. 'If he's such a great surgeon, why isn't he working? He doesn't seem to have anything on his mind other than gardening, fishing and generally enjoying his leisure time. Although…' She paused, thinking things through. 'Perhaps he's too worried about Francie to do anything else right now?' She guessed Francie must be his wife.

'Well, that could be the case, I suppose, but for whatever reason, he left his job down in Somerset and came up here with the boy. I thought perhaps he had decided our facilities were outstanding—we've certainly had a good star rating these last few years. But, whatever the reason, Admin would dearly like to get him on our team, even though he seems to be resisting at the moment.' He was already striding towards the exit. 'Must go.'

Megan stared after him. It was all very strange. Theo must be something very special for all this fuss to be created, and why would Theo be so resistant to persuasion that he would resort to making excuses? None of it made any sense at all.

'Would you take a look at the patient in room three?' a nurse asked, cutting into her thoughts. 'She's in some discomfort, with leg pain and some swelling, and I'm concerned that her condition is deteriorating. She appears to be a little breathless from some kind of chest infection, and her pulse oximetry reading is falling, so she's clearly not getting enough oxygen.'

'That doesn't sound too good. Has she been on a long-distance flight recently, or is there any history of stroke or heart disease?'

The nurse shook her head. 'She had surgery four weeks ago—a problem with fibroids in the womb.'

'OK, Beth, I'll take a look at her.' Megan was already walking in the direction of the examination room. 'Are you free to assist? It sounds as though she needs oxygen therapy.'

'Yes. I'll set that up, shall I?'

'Please do.'

Megan entered the room and cheerfully introduced herself

to the woman who was sitting on the bed, propped up by pillows. 'Mrs Baxter,' she said, glancing at the chart the nurse had prepared, 'would you like to tell me what the problem is?'

Sue Baxter showed her the area on her calf that was troubling her. 'It's very painful,' she told her. 'It seemed to come on quite suddenly.'

'It certainly looks as though it must be uncomfortable,' Megan agreed. 'You also have a low-grade fever, according to your chart.' She pulled her stethoscope from the pocket of her white jacket. 'I'll just need to listen to your chest, and we'll check your blood pressure once more. From the earlier reading it appears to be a touch low.' She quickly examined the woman and then gave her an encouraging smile. 'I'm going to take some blood for testing and arrange a special kind of CT scan so that we can see what's going on more clearly. In the meantime, we'll give you oxygen to help you breathe more easily.'

Going to the side of the room, she spoke in a low voice to the nurse. 'It looks as though there might be a blood clot forming in her vein, so I'm going to get her started on anti-coagulation therapy to prevent things from getting any worse. We need to get the CT scan done as soon as possible. The technician will inject a contrast dye into her blood vessels and that will show up any clots that have already formed.'

Some time later, after she had set up an intravenous line in her patient's arm, she said, 'I'll organise the scan and I'll be back to see you in a while, but in the meantime, please let the nurse know if your symptoms change or begin to get worse. We'll get you some compression stockings to see if that will help make you more comfortable, and I'm going to place a couple of pillows under your leg to raise it a little.'

Satisfied that she had done all she could for the time being, she spent the next hour or so dealing with a steady stream of patients, checking every now and again to see if any lab results had come back.

There was still no report from the CT technician, so she headed for the central area to see if she could hurry things up. Coming to a sudden halt, she was disconcerted to see that Theo Benyon was standing by the reception desk.

John Edwards's words came back to her… 'Don't let him escape.' But how was she supposed to keep him there when she had a job to do? Quickly, she paged her boss. His meeting would obviously have to take second place if this was so important to him.

'Hello again,' she said, going over to Theo, and he turned to look in her direction. His appearance had a decidedly unsettling effect on her. Long and lean, and once again immaculately dressed in a dark-coloured suit, he was lounging negligently against the desk, deep in conversation with the young nurse who was monitoring admissions there. She appeared to be basking in his attention.

'You're quite a frequent visitor around here, aren't you?' Megan added. 'Is there anything at all that I can do for you?'

His mouth tilted attractively. 'Now, there's a tempting proposition,' he murmured, his blue gaze moving over her. 'I'm sure I can think of all manner of things that might fit the bill.'

She pulled in a quick breath and pinned him with a cool, grey stare. Did the man have no shame? Even with his wife desperately ill in hospital, he was still prepared to try out his charm on all and sundry. Perhaps it came naturally to him, as easily as breathing air.

Her mind drifted back in time. Only the other day he had caused Sarah's cheeks to flush with warmth, hadn't he? And she couldn't help but notice that the nurse on reception duty was looking all of a flutter.

Well, he would find that *she* was one woman who wasn't going to be drawn by his magnetic lure. 'Of course it will be Mr Edwards that you're wanting to see,' she murmured, ignoring his remark. 'I've paged him, so he should be down here at any moment.'

His head went back a fraction. 'You didn't need to do that. All I want to do is drop off a couple of paintings that he asked for. If they're not suitable, he can easily let me know and I'll drop by and pick them up next time I'm here.'

She nodded. 'I guess you and Harry must be getting quite used to this place by now.' Glancing around, she discovered that there was no sign of his young son. 'Is Harry with his mother?' she asked.

He shook his head. 'Not today. Sometimes these visits can be upsetting for him, so I've been limiting the number of times I bring him along. Anyway, I've managed to enrol him in the local school, so at least he'll have the opportunity to make new friends, and it will help to keep his mind off what's going on here. He wasn't too happy about it, but all this change in his life has been unsettling for him, and he needs to get back to normality as much as possible.'

'Poor boy.' Megan's gaze clouded. 'I can imagine it must be difficult for both of you.' She frowned slightly, trying to make sense of what was going on. 'Mr Edwards told me that he had operated on Harry's mother. Is there any chance that she will make a quick recovery? Do you mind me asking? Only Mr Edwards didn't say what was wrong.'

Theo grimaced. 'Francie suffered a cerebral haemorrhage. It came on very suddenly when she complained of a terrible headache, like a blow to the head, and then she collapsed. It turned out that it was a burst blood vessel in her head and we were very worried that she wasn't going to make it. John was down in Somerset at the time on an exchange visit and offered to work with the team who operated on her. I'm sure it was his expertise that pulled her through.'

'I'm so sorry.' Megan was shocked. Many patients didn't survive such a devastating incident, and those who did often faced a long road back to health. 'How is she? Was the operation a success?'

'In the sense that she survived, I suppose so, yes.' He half turned away from her, as though he would hide the emotions that suddenly ravaged him, but she was watching him intently and she saw that his features had become shadowed, tinged with grief and regret. 'Of course, she's suffered badly as a result of the initial damage from the haemorrhage, and she's paralysed down one side, so that she can't walk, or use her arm, and her speech has been lost. The only consolation is that she's young, and that gives her a fighting chance for recovery.'

'That's why you brought her here, isn't it? So that she would be treated in the new stroke centre?'

'Yes.' He lifted his head, facing her once more. 'I heard about the work that was being done here, and I wanted her to have the very best of care…along with the fact that Harry's grandparents live near by. He needs their support right now. He's very young and he hasn't managed to come to terms with what has happened to his mother just yet.'

'That will probably take some time.'

He nodded. Then, as though he wanted to change the subject, he said briskly, 'About these paintings—I've stacked them behind the reception desk for the time being. Do you think you could let John know that they're here? Then I'll be on my way.'

'Oh, no…' Megan suddenly remembered that, quite apart from her own interest in this man, her boss was still hoping to speak to him. 'Do you really have to go right now? I mean, I was hoping that—' She broke off as the receptionist interrupted.

'Megan, a message has just come through for you from the CT technician,' Rhianna said. 'The scan showed a deep vein thrombosis, but as she was doing the scan, the patient's condition worsened. It looks as though a portion of the clot has broken off and travelled to her lung. She's having difficulty breathing and her heart rate is galloping.'

'Oh, Lord, that's the last thing we need.' Megan had to think quickly. 'Check that there's an operating room available for me, will you, Rhianna, and assemble a team? Ask Sarah to prep the patient for me. I'll have to do a pulmonary angiography to see if there's any way I can dissolve the clot.' She turned to Theo. 'Is there any chance at all that you could stay? I would have liked to talk to you about your paintings…'

It was true enough, but she could see that he was sceptical about that, and perhaps it would not be wise at this moment to remind him that her boss might put in an appearance any time soon. He didn't seem too keen on meeting up with him.

As a last desperate measure to keep him around, she tacked on, 'I don't suppose you'd care to come along with me, would you? I've heard about your expertise as a surgeon and I'd value your support if you would like to stand by in the operating theatre.' After all, he must be particularly brilliant if John Edwards spoke highly of him.

Theo's expression froze. 'Thanks, but, no, thanks. I really don't want to be anywhere near an operating theatre.'

'Oh…I didn't realise…' His remark threw her off kilter for a moment, but there was no time right now to query what he had said. She swallowed her disappointment. Her patient was in imminent danger and she had to get to her, fast. 'Please don't go away,' she said, moving away from the desk. 'I'm sure Rhianna will be glad to make you a cup of coffee and show you how our department works.' She glanced at the nurse for confirmation of that, and Rhianna nodded.

'Of course. I'll be happy to make coffee. We might even run to a piece of cake,' she added with a grin.

Megan hurried towards the operating theatre, her head filled with concern for her patient. The next hour would be crucial in determining whether the woman lived or died. Pulmonary embolisms could be devastating for anyone who suffered such an event, and if she didn't act quickly, her patient could go into cardiac arrest.

'Will you go in through the leg vein or her arm?' Sarah wanted to know, once Megan was ready to start the procedure.

'The groin, I think…the femoral vein,' Megan answered, 'and we'll monitor her blood pressure through the artery.' She braced herself and started the procedure. 'OK, I'm going to guide the catheter along the blood vessel and into the lung. Keep a check on her vital signs and let me know if there are any changes in heart rate or blood pressure.'

The procedure was a painstaking one, and for the next hour Megan needed all her powers of concentration to ensure that the catheter progressed through the woman's circulatory system without causing damage to the veins. Any puncture of the walls of a blood vessel could cause a massive bleed. Once in position, special instruments would help her to deal with the clot.

'Her circulation's improving,' Sarah said after a while, when Megan had almost finished, 'and her heart rate is dropping.'

'That's good. I'm ready to start withdrawing the catheter now.'

The procedure came to an end. Megan checked that Sue's breathing was easier and all her vital signs were showing im-

provement before she thanked the team for their help and left
the operating theatre.

She was keyed up, worried by how close she had come to
losing her patient, and she still had to go down to A and E to
check whether Theo Benyon had stayed around. Though
surely John Edwards would have come away from his meeting
by now. Somehow, after the gruelling hour she had just spent,
she was less enthusiastic about meeting up with Theo once
more. Maybe the intense concentration required by her work
had succeeded in bringing her securely down to earth. She
would do better to keep out of Theo's orbit.

Walking along the corridor, she glanced through the glass-
panelled door of the doctors' lounge and saw that her boss and
Theo were deep in conversation. That was a great relief. If her
boss had Theo in tow, she was off the hook, wasn't she? There
was no need after all for her to stay around and make polite
conversation.

'Ah, there you are, Megan. Come and join us, will you?'
John pulled open the door, stopping her in mid-stride when
she would have slipped silently by.

'I was just going to check up on my patients,' she
murmured, but John was having none of it.

'I'm certain you're due for a break,' he said. 'I expect the
senior house officer will manage perfectly well without you
for a while. I've told Theo that you'll take him on a tour of
the department—show him how we operate around here.
You'll be able to do that for me, won't you?' He glanced at
his watch. 'Only I have to go back to my management
meeting—matters of the hospital budget, you know. Dire
stuff, but it has to be done.'

'Oh, um…I thought…I was just…' Conscious that her
dismay must be showing and that she was babbling incoher-

ently, Megan made an effort to pull herself together. 'Yes, of course I can do that.'

Theo gave a wry smile. 'I really don't want to put you to any trouble. I know that you're busy, and I'm sure there are all sorts of other, more important, things that you need to be doing.'

'Nonsense,' John cut in firmly. 'She'll be only too happy to do it. Megan's our vascular specialist, you know. She's a brilliant asset to our A and E department...' He glanced at Megan. 'Haven't you just come from treating a patient for a pulmonary embolism? How did it go?'

Megan nodded. 'I have. It went well enough, I think. I managed to latch onto the clot with the instrumentation, and once I had it secured I infused it with clot-dissolving medication. When it reached a manageable size I was able to suck it up via the catheter and draw it out of her system. I'm hoping that we have her condition under control now.'

John gave a beaming smile. 'See, there we have it.' He threw Theo a quick glance. 'She's second to none, and I'm sure she'll be able to answer any question you care to put to her. I know I'll be leaving you in good hands.'

With that, her boss said a quick goodbye and headed for the door. 'Do let me know what you decide about the job,' he told Theo. 'We really want to have you on our team.'

Theo's expression was unreadable, and if John had been hoping for some sign that he had pulled him on board, he must have been sadly disappointed.

The door closed behind her boss, and Megan glanced at Theo. 'I feel that I should apologise for him,' she murmured. 'Around here, we tend to get used to his bombastic ways. He means well, but he does have a way of browbeating people from time to time.'

'That's all right. I'm sure he'll discover soon enough that

I can be equally determined when I've made up my mind on something,' he returned.

A perceptive glint shimmered in her eyes. 'I gather you still don't want the job?'

'No. I definitely don't want the job.'

'So there wouldn't be much point in my showing you around the department, then, would there?'

He shook his head. 'Not really.'

She sent him a thoughtful glance. 'So why did you stay here and let him talk your ears off? You were all for leaving over an hour ago, weren't you?'

'That's true, but you asked me not to go away, and even though I realise that might have been a ruse to delay me so that your boss could make his pitch, I thought perhaps if I stayed I might at least be able to persuade you to have dinner with me this evening.'

She took a sharp intake of breath. Had he really stayed simply because she'd asked him to? For a dizzying moment her head reeled with the full import of that. Perhaps in some way he was as taken with her as she was intrigued by him. Why else would he be asking her out to dinner?

But then reality descended on her like a dark cloud. The man wasn't free to ask her out, was he? Did he have no shame?

'Mr Benyon,' she said in a tight voice, 'I don't quite know how to put this politely, but I have to say that I think it's in very poor taste for you to be asking me out when your wife is desperately ill in hospital.'

He stared at her for a moment without saying anything at all. His blue gaze skimmed over her, taking in the smoke grey of her eyes and coming to linger on the firm tilt of her chin. Then, very quietly, he said, 'I take it that's a no, then?'

'It certainly is. That's a...read my lips...definite no.'

'Hmm.' He studied her thoughtfully. 'You know, you're really very uptight and overwrought for someone so young. It shows in the stiff line of your shoulders and in the way you move, as though you have to make every second count. I can't help thinking that it might do you a world of good if you could manage to loosen up just a little.'

She blinked, taken aback by his blunt assessment. 'You're entitled to your opinion,' she told him, 'but the plain fact is I have a job to do, and it's work that I enjoy, and feel privileged to take on, even if you seem to take the opposite view.' She frowned. 'Of course, I understand that your wife's condition must be playing on your mind to some extent right now, and you have Harry to look after. Perhaps that's why you don't feel like considering John's offer.'

'I appreciate your concern,' he murmured, 'however misplaced it might be. Of course I'm worried about Francie's condition. What happened to her doesn't bear thinking about, and it was extremely difficult for me to come to terms with the events that followed. The truth is, though, Francie is my sister, not my wife, and if you weren't quite so wound up with the job and everything that goes along with it, you might have taken time out to think things through, and then you probably wouldn't have jumped to conclusions quite so readily.'

Megan felt her throat close up, leaving her speechless. She was stunned by his revelation. Had she really done it again and jumped in with both feet before looking where she was going?

He walked over to the door. 'I'll leave you to your patients,' he said, his tone dry. 'I'm sure they'll do wonderfully well under all your lavish attention.'

She watched him pull open the door. He was going, he was actually moving away from her without a second thought, and it was what she deserved after snubbing him that way, wasn't it? Why did she have to go and speak her mind before checking that she had her facts right?

'I had no idea,' she managed, her voice thready.

'No, I see that.' His mouth made a wry shape. 'Perhaps you should just remember to leave a little time for yourself every now and again. It's what makes people human.'

CHAPTER FOUR

'WHAT do you mean, he left without seeing round the department?' John's dark brows rose with alarming precision. 'I thought you were going to do your best to work your charm on him?'

'Yes, well…unfortunately, he had other plans.' Megan had no idea how she could begin to appease her boss. 'The truth is, I really don't think he wants to work here. I'm not sure that he wants to work anywhere. In fact, he doesn't appear to want to even go anywhere near an operating theatre.'

'Then you have to find out why.' John was frowning heavily. 'You seem to get along with him well enough, and you've spoken to the boy, Harry. See what you can do to put things right next time you see him. He's bound to be coming in to visit the child's mother before too long. I'm relying on you, Megan.' He patted her shoulder in an avuncular fashion. 'You can sweet-talk him, I know you can.'

Megan did her best not to scowl. 'John, you don't seem to understand how it is. I don't know why you imagine I can do anything to bring him round to your way of thinking. He doesn't have a very high opinion of me.'

'Of course he does.' John shook his head. 'No one can possibly think badly of you. Tell him about your ambulance project. He's bound to see the sense in it. Anyone can see how important it is that we have skilled doctors going along with the ambulance crew on long-haul journeys with critically ill patients. He's bound to want to know more about it and, who knows, he might even offer to lend his support. That would be a feather in our cap. He's at the top of his field. People will sit up and take notice.'

Megan silently ground her teeth together. Why was she surrounded by men who always thought they knew best? Why would he never listen?

She said quietly, 'I'm going to take these fliers about the project and hand them round to staff so that they can distribute them in GP practices and walk-in centres in the town and local villages. If we can persuade just one doctor to volunteer to be on call with the ambulance for high-priority, emergency transport to hospital, it might help to save lives. I've lost count of the number of people who might have been saved if they'd had specialist attention from the moment of collapse. These long-haul journeys to hospital can have a disastrous outcome for seriously ill people from outlying areas.'

'You're right, of course.' He was nodding vigorously. 'There's a national network of volunteers to serve most of the country, but unfortunately our rural area has somehow missed out. It's a good thing you're doing there, Megan. Keep up the good work.'

He moved off at a brisk pace to attend to his paperwork, leaving Megan to stare after him. Why was he laying the problem of Theo Benyon at her feet? He was the last person on earth she wanted to deal with. What was it Theo had said...she was uptight...stiff and in need of loosening up? His words still had the power to cut her to the quick. So she cared deeply about her work. Why was that a problem? Surely it was better than giving up on it altogether as he had done?

Still, his antipathy towards the job was very odd. Had he something else in mind, another job lined up in a different hospital? That would really serve to ruffle John's feathers, wouldn't it? And she wouldn't give three guesses as to who would get the blame for letting him slip away.

She sighed. Maybe, for the sake of her peace of mind, she ought to at least make an effort to seek Theo out and apologise for her misunderstanding of his situation. Unfortunately, the prospect filled her with dismay, so that she relegated it to the very last item on her agenda. She was more than happy to put it off for a while.

She went, instead, to examine her next patient, a man in his thirties, who shifted restlessly on the bed and had a faint sheen of sweat on his brow.

'Mr Langton was bitten by a dog a few days ago,' Beth told her. 'He's complaining of soreness in his leg around the area of the bite, but he also has more generalised symptoms that are making him feel very unwell. He's feverish, too.'

Megan glanced at the man's chart. 'Your heart rate is fast, Mr Langton, and your blood pressure is low, according to this,' she murmured, glancing at him. Going over to the bedside, she could see that his breathing was compromised, too, the air being pulled into his lungs in short, fast gulps.

'Your leg looks very sore,' she commented as she noted the redness and swelling around the wound. 'It looks as though an infection has set in.' Streaks of red were spreading like fingers upwards from the affected area.

Mr Langton nodded. 'I've a headache, and I'm feeling sick. Is there something you can give me that will put things right?'

Megan nodded. 'We'll take some blood for testing, but in the meantime Beth will give you an injection of a wide-spectrum antibiotic to try to put a stop to the infection, along with something to help with the pain. I'm afraid we're going to have to admit you for a day or two, so that we can continue to give you intravenous antibiotics until the condition is brought under control.'

He winced. 'I bathed the leg after the bite, but I didn't realise it was that bad until I started to get chills. It all seemed to come on in the last day or so.'

Megan gave him a sympathetic smile. 'You're not a postman, by any chance, are you? Dog bites seem to be one of the hazards of the job.'

He shook his head. 'It was a mate's dog that did this. He's always been fine with me when I call to the house but then out of the blue he bit me. Talk about unpredictable.'

'It happens like that sometimes,' Megan said. 'Well, we'll do our best to make you more comfortable. Just rest for a while and I'll go and organise your admission to the medical ward.'

By the end of the afternoon she was ready to finish her shift, but Rhianna called out to her from the reception desk as she was preparing to leave.

'There you are, Megan—I was just about to page you. Mr Edwards asked me to let you know when Mr Benyon was coming in. He'll be along any minute now, apparently—he's just rung through to say that he'll sign the paperwork to release his paintings to us now that the boss has decided that they are what we want for the waiting-room area. He thought that perhaps you would show him where they are to be displayed.'

Megan did her best to hide her frustration. She might have known that John wouldn't leave anything to chance.

'I suppose I'd better stay and have a word with him, then.'

She stopped by the desk and riffled through the paperwork in the wire tray, looking for lab-test results. 'I might as well sign off some of the charts while I'm here. Mr Edwards can have the pleasure of looking through them first thing in the morning.'

Rhianna gave a smile and a few minutes later said softly, 'Here's your man now.'

Her man? The words gave her a jolt. Heaven forbid. Megan looked up from her charts and braced herself as Theo walked towards the desk. He was smartly dressed, as usual, this time wearing dark trousers and a crisply laundered shirt, with his jacket hanging loose. His tie was a subtle blend of grey-blue that reminded her of the colour of his eyes, and compelled her own eyes towards his face.

He appeared to be preoccupied, but for a brief moment as his gaze meshed with hers his eyes took on an alert expression, a glitter of recognition that pierced her to the core. Then he seemed to get a hold of himself, and merely nodded briefly in her direction, turning away to enquire pleasantly of Rhianna about the paperwork he was to sign.

That was not a good beginning, and Megan struggled to interpret what he must have been thinking in that transitory moment of contact. Most likely he was still annoyed with her about the way she had jumped to conclusions about him.

'It's all here, ready for you,' the receptionist murmured. 'Mr Edwards thought it would be a good idea if Megan was to show you where he decided to put the paintings since he isn't here to greet you himself. He thought perhaps you would like to come back next week and see them in pride of place.'

'I might, if I didn't suspect that was another ploy on his part.' He took a pen from his jacket pocket and added his signature to the papers in a bold, flowing hand. Then he turned to Megan. 'There's no need for you to show me around, you know. I've already seen the areas he had in mind.'

She inclined her head briefly. 'It won't take more than a

minute or two, and it's no trouble at all. I've finished my shift for the day, and I was hoping that I would be able to talk to you, anyway.'

He sent her a doubtful glance. 'Really? I thought we'd said all that needed to be said. Or, rather, you did. We both know where we stand, don't we?'

'Do we?' Megan winced. Was he still put out by the way she had attempted to shoot him down in flames? There must be some way that she could put that right, surely?

She threw a quick farewell glance in Rhianna's direction as she started to lead him away from the reception area, and the receptionist returned the look with a slight wave.

'I expect you've been to see your sister,' Megan guessed as she walked with Theo towards the patients' waiting area. 'How is she doing? Has there been any progress at all?'

'Nothing spectacular,' he said. 'As you can imagine, these things take time, and at the moment she's still suffering the after-effects of surgery. The team looking after her is hoping to start her on a regular programme of physiotherapy soon to help her to regain the use of her arm and leg, but progress is likely to be very slow. The speech therapist has been to see her and she'll be doing what she can to help her to learn to talk again.'

He grimaced. 'At least we know that she understands what people are saying, and she's able to write things down with her good hand. She doesn't always manage to choose the correct words, but generally she manages to make herself understood.'

'I'm sorry. It must be really difficult for you to stand by and see her struggle that way.'

His features were shadowed. 'It isn't easy, but I'd say it was more of a problem for Harry. He misses his mother desperately.'

'Yes. I'm sure he does.' Megan hesitated, not wanting to add to his sorrow in any way. 'That must make it all the more worrying for you.'

By now they had reached the waiting area, and she paused, glancing around. 'This is the first section that Mr Edwards had in mind for your countryside landscape.' She waved a hand towards the bare wall. 'We thought the image of the stream bubbling gently over rocks into a woodland pool would be calming for the patients if we placed it here.' She looked to him for approval, and he nodded briefly.

'I can see how that would work.' He made a faint smile of acknowledgement and her spirits lifted a fraction.

'The second area is beyond here, on a wall that faces the treatment bays,' she told him, leading the way towards the cubicled section. 'When the curtains are open, patients will be able to look out on to your tropical beach scene. We felt that the vision of palm trees and white surf breaking on the sand would make them think of happier times and perhaps take their minds off their troubles.'

He nodded. 'I'm glad that they'll be put to a useful purpose.'

'They will.' She was curious about his generosity towards the hospital, and it prompted her to say quietly, 'We are very grateful to you, you know. I don't think many trust authorities would have received such a selfless offer as yours. You haven't asked for payment of any kind, have you?'

Theo shrugged. 'As far as I'm concerned, it'll be thanks enough if people find pleasure in looking at my work. I never intended to make a living from it.'

'No…but, as I said before, I'm sure you could, if that's what you wanted.' She sent him a quick, thoughtful glance. 'I have to say I'm intrigued by how you are able to simply turn your back on the medical profession. John speaks very highly of you. He says you can be counted as one of the best surgeons around...in fact, he considers you to be second to none.'

Theo gave her an odd look. 'You really don't need to try to butter me up. It won't make any difference in the long run. I still don't have any plans to come and work here.'

Megan gave a slight gasp of dismay. 'No...no, you have it all wrong. I wasn't trying to flatter you, truly I wasn't. I suppose, if anything, I was simply saying that I find it hard to understand what it is that makes you tick.'

What she was saying was the truth, she realised. For some reason that defied logic, she was becoming more and more fascinated by this man and his lifestyle. What would make a gifted surgeon turn his back on his career? Could it simply be that he wanted to look out for his young nephew? She had to admire him for the sense of responsibility that had led him to do that.

'Maybe you should give up on trying to understand what makes me tick,' he said, adding on a note of self-derision, 'I'm not altogether sure that I could fully explain it myself.' He smiled self-derisively.

She tilted her head to one side, gazing at him, her expression curious, the silky swirl of her chestnut hair coming to rest lightly on her shoulders.

'You're being very gracious towards me, all things considered,' she said after a second or two. 'I'm not sure I deserve such generous treatment from you. I've done nothing but make judgements about you from the moment we first met, and I'm sorry for that. I was totally in the wrong. I was hoping that you might find it in you to forgive me.'

He made a wry face. 'I forgive you. Perhaps I was a little touchy. The thing is, I'm taking time out to take stock of everything that's happened over the last few months and it seems to me that everyone wants a piece of me or has an opinion about what I should be doing.' His shoulders moved in a negligent fashion. 'In fact, it's nobody's business but mine.'

She nodded, feeling a strange kind of empathy towards him. 'Yes, that's true…and I've been one of those people, haven't I?' Her grey eyes were thoughtful as she studied him. 'Is there any way I can redeem myself? It was wrong of me to assume that you were married and had a child, but it was a genuine mistake. I can only say that it's probably true what you said, that I lose myself in my work to the detriment of all else.'

She made a vague gesture with her hands, indicating their surroundings. 'In a way, the A and E department here is like my second home. My colleagues and the patients are almost like family to me.'

Her mouth made a faint, downward turn. In truth, weren't they her only family, the only people who cared? Working here had given her stability that she'd never known before, and the friendship and loyalty she'd discovered here had helped to make up for all the bad times that had gone before.

He sent her an oblique glance. 'Now, that makes me even more curious about you. Perhaps you're not everything that you project to the outside world, are you? In a way, that makes us two of a kind.'

'Does it?'

He nodded. 'I believe so…and if you mean what you say about wanting to make up for your hasty assumptions, I dare say there is one thing that you could do for me.'

Her eyes widened. 'And that is?'

'You could help me out with something. Of course, you're perfectly free to say no.'

Something about the way he was looking at her put her immediately on her guard. His expression was bland, as though he didn't much care either way, but at the same time a spark of flame had come to life in his eyes and seemed to belie his intent.

Megan took a moment before she answered him. She had made too many wrong guesses about him already, and she was loath to compound her mistakes by treating his offer as suspicious from the outset.

'What did you have in mind?'

'Nothing too difficult…so you don't need to look so worried.' Again, there was that smile that lit up his face. 'It's just that I need someone to advise me on what to do about the furnishings for my new house—well, it isn't new, as such, but it will be my home for the time being. I'm taking over my grandparents' old house for the next few months, while I'm here in Wales, and it's so cluttered up with bits and pieces of furniture that I'm not sure where to start with sorting things out. I thought maybe you might like to help.'

'Oh, I see.' Megan wasn't sure how to respond. This wasn't at all what she had been expecting. Was he serious? Perhaps he was just hoping for a woman's touch about the place, a helping hand with making a house into a home?

'Why me? I'm not sure that my instincts would be any better than yours.'

His mouth curved. 'Two heads are better than one, as they say, and you're a woman, which in my book puts you streets ahead with this kind of thing. Women generally have a flair for homemaking.' He sent her a mischievous look. 'Besides, I still have a yen to get to know you better. Even with all that's going on in my life, I feel that some things are definitely worth pursuing.'

He wanted to spend time with her? Megan's eyes widened a fraction. It appeared to be true enough. He was looking at her in a way that sent the blood fizzing through her veins and warmed her from head to toe, and she could only hope that there wasn't a corresponding rush of colour to go along with the tide of heat that flooded her cheeks.

How should she answer him? Hadn't she told herself she would steer clear of men and any kind of entanglement, given the way life conspired to let her down time and again? Yet here she was contemplating the idea of getting to know Theo better.

Still, she had jumped to conclusions about him twice already, and surely this wasn't too much for him to ask of her? It would be the least she could do to try to make amends, and agreeing to help him out wouldn't mean that she was committing herself to anything else, would it?

'I'm willing to give it a try,' she told him after a while. 'Are your grandparents no longer around, or are they away for a while?'

'They passed on some time ago. I inherited the house from them—or, rather, my parents did, and eventually it was turned over to me. We want to keep it in the family, since there are so many good memories associated with it. I decided that we might all use it as a holiday home, somewhere we could stay from time to time, as and when we needed it. Of course, there's always the possibility of renting it out to holidaymakers in the summers, but I haven't made any decision about that as yet.'

She smiled. 'That sounds like a lovely idea, especially keeping it for the family. I gather no one has used it up to now?'

'That's right, but we decided that it would be the ideal place for me to stay when I moved up here from Somerset.'

'Did you have your own place back there?'

He nodded. 'Still do. I thought it best to hold onto the property in Taunton in case I make up my mind to go back one day.'

She sent him a quick glance. 'Is that likely?'

'I'm not sure. The hospital where I worked wants me to go back at some point, but I prefer to keep my options open. Right now, it's the very last thing I want to do and, anyway, I need to concentrate on Harry and Francie and their needs. In the meantime, I've rented the property out for a few months.'

He waved a hand towards the exit doors. 'Shall we go? Didn't you say you had finished your shift for the day? I could drive you over there right now, if you have the time, and if that's OK with you?'

'Yes, I'm free to do that, but I think I'd rather follow you in my own car, thanks all the same. That way I can make my way home later.'

He nodded. 'As you please. We take the road from here and head towards Llansannan. The house is in a village in the Cledwen Valley, some five miles or so from Betws-y-Coed. Will that take you too far away from where you're living?'

'Actually, no, from the sound of things, it won't. My house is just off that same road. I live in a village that's quite close to the reservoir.'

'That's good, then.' He smiled. 'It looks as though we live reasonably close to one another.'

He led the way out to the car park, moving at a brisk pace and giving her no time at all to even think of changing her mind.

On the drive over there she had time to think about the fact that she could be making a big mistake. Nothing had gone right in their tenuous relationship so far, and it could well be that he would discount any of her ideas for making his house liveable. What was he expecting from her?

At least the familiar journey through the lush countryside served in part to soothe some of her worries away. She drove through quiet, wooded valleys, passing by picturesque villages along the way, and in the distance there was the backdrop of sloping hills and magnificent mountain ranges to calm her down.

It wasn't long, though, before Theo turned his silver saloon off the country road they were following to take a narrow lane instead, and after a while she saw that he was heading towards what looked like an isolated farmhouse. As he slowed down and eased the vehicle along the driveway, she realised that this must be his grandparents' former home.

It was built of stone, a large building that boasted two deeply pitched roofs, with a lower dormer roof between them. Drawing her own car to a halt in front of the house, she studied it thoughtfully. The simplicity of the design was easy on the eye, and she loved the symmetry of it, along with the mellowed stone, the wide front porch and the mullioned windows that were carved in an aesthetically pleasing way and seemed to hark back to earlier centuries. There was something about the house that spoke of quiet grandeur, family living and understated wealth.

Theo came over and held open the car door for her as she began to slide out from the driver's seat.

'This is it,' he said. 'What do you think of the place—first impressions and so on?'

'It's lovely,' she said, gazing at the house in wonder. 'Truly impressive. I can understand why you wanted to keep it in the family. At first, when we approached it from a distance, I thought maybe it was a farmhouse, but I imagine it was more of a country retreat.'

He appeared to relax a fraction, and she guessed that he was pleased with her observations. 'I suppose it was a bit of both, really. My great-grandparents farmed the land hereabouts for a time. They grew crops and herded sheep, but all that finished long ago.'

'Won't you rattle about in it, living here all by yourself?'

She stopped herself, and tacked on, 'But perhaps I have that all wrong. I guess I'm prone to jumping in without thinking.'

He laughed softly. 'It's all right. You're forgiven.' He watched as she locked up her car and then led the way towards the house, the palm of his hand resting lightly in the small of her back and stirring up all kinds of responses within her. It was such a gentle touch, light and unassuming but protective and guiding all at once. Warmth surged through her veins, spreading out from her spine and filling every part of her being. She wasn't sure what prompted her to feel this way, but there was something about this man that heightened all her senses. Just being near to him was enough to raise her awareness to unprecedented levels.

'As a matter of fact,' he added as he unlocked the front door, 'Harry is living here with me while his mother is in hospital, but you're right in thinking that the place is too big for the two of us. It's a house meant for a large family...although Harry loves to explore all the rooms. He likes the space.'

'I can imagine.' She looked around the wide hallway. 'It's so light in here. I hadn't expected that somehow, but the sunlight seems to pour in...the windows are long and wide, aren't they?'

'That's one of the beauties of this house. It's set in its own grounds and the aspect is just perfect. I even have one room set aside as a studio.'

Her mouth curved. 'That must be one of the great attractions of the place for you. I expect you can shut yourself away in the garret and paint to your heart's content.' She could imagine him doing just that, the artist in him locked away from the distractions of the world, driven by the passion of his vision.

He gave her a crooked smile. 'The theory's good, but unfortunately Harry demands a lot of attention. He doesn't have the patience to hang around while I follow my creative urges.'

'Does he not stay with his grandparents at all?' She followed him into a large reception room, where two cream-coloured sofas and a wooden dresser vied for space with a rectangular dining table and chairs made out of solid oak. She frowned. 'I see what you mean about clutter. This is a magnificent room, but the furniture makes it look crowded.'

'It does.' His glance swept the room. 'As to Harry, he's with my parents at the moment. They love to have him stay with them, but he's been a bit of a handful lately with everything that's gone on, so I don't leave him there too long.'

'Are there no maternal grandparents?'

He shook his head. 'I'm afraid not...and as to Harry's father, he didn't stay around long enough to find out that he had a son. He was always on the move, ready for the next challenge, and Francie paid the price of falling for him. After he left, she made up her mind that there was no point in telling him about Harry.'

'I'm sorry. That must have been difficult for her.'

'Yes, but she was always a survivor. She worked hard to build a career for herself in designing children's clothes, and that meant she could work from home and take care of Harry at the same time. Of course, all that has come to an abrupt end now.'

Megan's glance skimmed his features. 'In one way she's fortunate, in that she has a brother who is willing to step in and help out. It must be an enormous comfort to her.'

He shrugged. 'Francie and I were always close. I've only done what others would do for their families in similar circumstances.'

'Even so, I'm not altogether sure that many people would be so wholehearted in their response.' It would be good to think that human kindness was in abundance all around, but her own experience led her to think otherwise. Perhaps Theo was a very special breed of man.

He looked at her oddly. 'You sound disillusioned. Have things not always gone the way you might have hoped?'

'I tend not to hope for anything. I'm a realist. I see life as it is. All I'm saying is that not many people would give up their career in order to care for someone dear to them. I imagine few people would be able to afford to.'

He frowned. 'I didn't give up my career for Francie.'

'You didn't?'

'No. I had already made up my mind to quit when she was taken ill.' He walked over to the door. 'Let me show you the rest of the house. There's another reception room across the hall from this one, and upstairs there are four bedrooms and the room that I've commandeered for my studio.'

Megan realised that she must have touched on a raw nerve and she decided not to pursue the subject of his career. 'I'd love to see that… I've been hoping that I might see some more of your paintings.'

He made a wry smile. 'You might not like them.'

Megan doubted that. From what she had seen of his landscapes for the hospital and the painting he had been working on by the canal, he appeared to have a sure touch. He obviously had a clear vision of what was in front of him and somehow he managed to transfer that perfectly to canvas. Perhaps that clarity of vision and deft handiwork was what made him such a good surgeon.

The studio was upstairs, at the back of the house, a well-proportioned room with deep windows on two sides and perfect light for the work he was doing. There were paintings all around, and she was surprised to find that there were portraits among them.

'I didn't realise that you painted people, too,' she murmured, her gaze going from one canvas to another. Her mouth curved. 'That's Harry, isn't it? A little younger, and his hair is longer than it is now, but it's definitely him.'

He nodded. 'I had to make several quick sketches before I could do the painting. The trouble is, Harry is never still for more than a second or two at a time.'

'I can imagine. It must be difficult to capture someone's likeness, but you've done it perfectly.' She gazed at the portrait for a little longer. 'His eyes have that look of expectation in them, a look that says, You'd better watch out, because I've just decided what I'm going to do next.'

He laughed. 'That's our Harry.'

Her gaze travelled to the next canvas, a full-length study of a pretty, dark-haired young woman who was seated by a table, carefully checking out a length of material. 'That must be your sister,' she said softly, looking at Theo for confirmation.

He nodded. 'I made that a couple of years ago. I wanted to do one of her with Harry, but I never quite managed to find the time.' His mouth flattened.

'She's lovely.' Megan sent him a brief, thoughtful glance. 'I'm sure you'll get the chance to do that painting. She's survived her operation and she's in the best place to make a good recovery. It will take time, but she's young and she'll come through this.'

'I wish I could be certain of that.' He turned away from the painting as though it was too painful for him to look at it any longer. 'There's just one room left to show you… I left the kitchen until last. I think you'll probably fall in love with it. It's the best room by far—the one room that has been completely renovated.'

Megan wondered if she ought not to have commented on

his sister's illness. He was troubled by what had happened to her, and she had only managed to stir things up again.

He was quiet as he led the way downstairs and along the corridor towards the kitchen, but as he opened the door and ushered her into the room, he sent her a quick glance, as though to gauge her reaction.

Gazing around, she gave a small gasp of delight. 'It's a perfect country kitchen,' she exclaimed softly, 'with the pale coloured beams, along with all these golden oak cupboards and the beautiful range cooker… It's wonderful.' She smiled. 'The decorative woodwork is lovely, too. It adds a beautiful touch to the shelving. It's fantastic.'

'I'm glad you approve.' His mouth made a brief upward slant. 'As we're in the right place, why don't I make us a pot of tea and offer you something to eat? I expect you haven't eaten since lunchtime, have you?'

'That's true. I'm actually quite hungry, but…' She stopped herself. 'I really don't want to put you to any trouble.'

'It's no trouble at all. I can do a pizza for you, and pop on some oven chips, and there's salad already prepared in the fridge. Does that sound OK?'

'More than OK. Is there anything I can do to help?'

He tilted his head towards the shelving. 'Maybe you could set out cups and saucers and cutlery? This shouldn't take too long to prepare, and we'll eat in here at the breakfast table in the corner.' He was already switching on the oven.

He removed his jacket, laying it over the back of a chair, and then went to wash his hands at the sink. Megan followed suit, rinsing her hands at the tap, and then she set about laying the small, circular table in readiness for the meal.

All the time she was conscious of his long, lean body as he moved about the kitchen. He was flat stomached, with broad shoulders, and when he rolled back the sleeves of his shirt she saw that his arms were a faint shade of golden brown. He was irresistibly male, a man who would melt any woman's heart.

Unnerved by his strong masculine presence, she sought something to do, filling the kettle with water and waiting for it to boil.

'You spoke earlier about leaving your job,' she murmured. 'Was there some special reason that you decided to quit?' Her grey eyes were troubled. 'Do you mind me asking?'

He shook his head. 'I know it must be hard to understand, and people are curious about my attitude.' He sprinkled extra grated cheese on top of the pizzas and added sliced tomato and mushrooms. 'All I can say is that it was something that came on me over a period of time.'

He took a moment to place the pizza and a tray of chips in the hot oven and then turned to face her. 'For years I've been treating patients to the best of my ability, fixing their damaged bodies, repairing their hearts and circulatory systems when things have gone wrong. I've always done everything that I can to try to save their lives, but increasingly it has dawned on me that there's only so much I can do to put things right. It grieves me when I see people too late, when the damage has been done and there's nothing more I can do for them. And one day I walked out of the operating theatre and thought, I can't do this any more. I'm through.'

Her gaze softened. 'I think we all feel like that from time to time. We battle against the odds and do what we can, but there are times when we are bound to fail.'

'I can't live with that. I knew it was time to get out when I started to wake up at night in a sweat because I dreamed I'd tried to operate with fingers that were numb and arms dragging as though they were made of lead.'

'I didn't realise.' Megan studied his anguished features. 'Did the nightmares happen very often?'

'Most nights. They don't happen so frequently now.'

'That must have been dreadful for you.'

'It was a sense of frustration that held me back more than anything. I wanted to try out new, lifesaving techniques, but I couldn't help feeling that the system was against me. We stick with what has been tried and tested, but it doesn't always work as it's supposed to. There's only so much we can do, and ultimately the patients are the ones who suffer.'

He looked so bereft that Megan couldn't help but feel a surge of compassion. She went over to him, wanting only to ease his pain and show him that he did not have to bear it alone. 'You do what you can. Why focus on the negative? Surely it's better to help a great number of people than none at all?' She laid a hand lightly on his arm, moving to be closer to him, and felt the muscles bunch involuntarily beneath her fingers.

She almost drew back, wondering if he resented her nearness, but in that moment he turned so that his body was in intimate, immediate contact with hers, and she felt a wild flush of response reverberate throughout her nervous system. Every cell in her body tingled, clamouring for more.

His breathing changed, became ragged, as though he, too, was affected by their closeness, and he gave a soft, husky sigh. 'You're very sweet,' he murmured, his fingers lifting to gently cup her jaw. He lightly tilted her face upwards, gazing all the while into her troubled grey eyes. His head bent towards her, and for a long, breathless moment she thought he might be about to kiss her.

But then he paused and instead gave her a fleeting, rueful smile as though he had thought better of it. 'My mind is made up, though,' he said softly, reluctantly moving away from her. 'I'm through with surgery.'

She felt a swift pulse of disappointment run through her as the closeness came to an end.

He straightened, turning back towards the cooker. 'My only priority right now is to feed you. I think these pizzas are ready.'

CHAPTER FIVE

'YOU went to his house?' Rhianna stared at Megan, her hazel eyes widening. 'The last time I saw you and Theo together you didn't appear to be getting along too well. Have things changed?'

Megan sidestepped the question. 'I think both of us were feeling wary, one way or another. We're on much better terms now, but he isn't an easy person to get to know, and I suppose I might be equally difficult.'

She smiled crookedly. 'Actually, he asked me if I would help him sort out the furnishings in the house, and when I saw it, I could understand why. It's quite beautiful, but some of the décor is a bit dated, in the second reception room and the small fourth bedroom upstairs especially. Added to that, there's so much furniture that he's inherited cluttering every room, and it's hard to see how it could be made just right for his own taste. I think some of the pieces are quite valuable, and he doesn't really want to get rid of them.'

'So have you managed to come up with some ideas?'

'I'm still working on it. I said that I would go back there this evening so that we could make a start.'

'Oh, yes?' Rhianna gave her a knowing look. 'You should watch yourself. Sounds as though he has an ulterior motive to me.'

Megan raised her brow. 'Why would you assume that?'

Rhianna shook her head. 'You're a hopeless case, aren't you? Anyone can see that he's attracted to you. Why else would he be hanging around?'

'Because he cares about his sister.' Megan was equally firm in her denial, but even as she spoke she felt a flush of heat flood her cheeks, and she lowered her head, hiding her expression with a swathe of silky hair. Theo may have said he wanted to get to know her better, but he had other priorities right now, hadn't he? Why else had he drawn back from her?

'If she wasn't being treated here in the stroke unit,' she added, 'we wouldn't be seeing anything of him, believe me.'

'Foolish girl.' Rhianna reached for the phone as the indicator light flashed. 'Borderlands A and E,' she said. 'How may I help?'

Megan turned away, leaving her to it. Rhianna had things all wrong. Theo was new to the area and was asking for advice, that was all. He had enough to contend with, having his sister ill in hospital and a child to look after. No matter what he said, they took precedence over everything, and that was fine as far as she was concerned, wasn't it? Given the definite charm he exuded, it would be all too easy to allow herself to be drawn to him, but that would be folly. Instinct warned her that she had to keep a sense of self-preservation in place.

Picking up a chart, she went along to the treatment room and prepared to see her next patient.

Beth was already there, making temperature, blood pressure and pulse observations, and she glanced across the room as Megan entered. 'Hello, there,' she said. 'I thought you would have left by now. Aren't you on call for the ambulance service this afternoon?'

Megan nodded. 'I thought I'd have time to see one last

patient before I hand over.' She glanced briefly at the chart, and then looked at the man lying on the bed. He looked as though he was in extreme discomfort. 'I understand that you have severe pain in the lower back…is that so?'

'That's right.'

'OK, let's see if we can find out what's causing the problem. Perhaps I could do a quick examination?' she suggested.

He nodded. 'It's really bad…a sharp, stabbing pain. I don't think I can stand it for much longer.'

'I'll give you something for the pain,' Megan said. After she had examined him and questioned him for a while, she told him, 'It looks as though it could be a kidney stone that's causing the problem, but we'll need to do a scan to confirm that. I'll organise it for you right away.'

'Thanks. What will happen if it is a stone?'

'That would depend on the size of it and whether or not it's causing an infection. If it's small, we could give you painkillers and wait to see if it passes out of you in the normal way. Otherwise we might opt to disperse it by using shock-wave treatment to break it up into tiny crystals, or possibly treat it surgically. We'll know more when we have the results of all the tests.'

Just a short time later, when she had done everything she could and handed over to the doctor who would be taking over her casework, she left the hospital and set off for home.

Living where she did, in a rural area, it meant that if any critically injured patients needed support on their way to hospital, she was already close by and would be ready and available to help out in an emergency. Her on-call time came around on a regular basis, but if she could enlist more doctors to help out, more people might benefit.

Was there any chance at all that Theo would want to help

out? It was doubtful, but from all that her boss had told her about him, he would make an excellent addition to the team. Rhianna might think that Theo had an ulterior motive in seeking her out, but wasn't *she* also working on the gem of an idea where Theo was concerned? Surely it would be best for him to get back to doing what he was skilled at before he lost his confidence altogether? Maybe she could help him with that?

'I'm sorry I'm later than I said,' she told him when she when she arrived at his house later that evening. 'I've been out with the ambulance, and things took longer than we bargained for.'

'That's OK. I guessed something important must have been keeping you.' He smiled, as though he was pleased to see her, his features lighting up, his blue eyes taking on a warm glow. He was dressed in casual clothes, chinos coupled with a loose-fitting shirt, and he managed to look comfortable and stylish at the same time.

'I'm glad you were able to make it,' he said. 'Come on in.' He opened the door wider and ushered her into the house. 'I've just made a pot of coffee and cut some sandwiches. Come through to the kitchen and help yourself...that's supposing that Harry has left some for you.'

Her gaze softened. 'I wondered if he would be here.'

Megan followed Theo into the kitchen and saw that Harry was sitting at the table by the window. He was playing with a toy racing-car, and in between skidding it around the teacups on two wheels he was taking bites out of a cheese sandwich.

'Hello, Harry.' She sent him a quick smile. 'How are you?'

He lifted his shoulders in a negligent shrug, and then glanced at her thoughtfully. 'You're the lady doctor from the hospital, aren't you?'

'That's right, I am. It's good to see you again.' She used a cheerful, encouraging tone, but he was unresponsive, so she turned her attention to his toy. 'Wow...that's a magnificent car... A midnight-blue Porsche. I wish I had one of those to drive around in.'

His features brightened. 'The doors open, and the bonnet lifts up...see?' He demonstrated, thrusting the car closer to her so that she could take a good look.

'It's wonderful. And you even have a man that fits in the driver's seat. That makes it extra-special, doesn't it?'

He nodded. 'My mum bought me the car...for my birthday.' His eyes clouded and his mouth turned down at the corners. 'She was going to buy me a man for it as a treat for when I started school, but then she was sick and had to go to hospital...so Uncle Theo bought him for me instead.'

'So you didn't miss out after all?' She glanced fleetingly at Theo. He was obviously tuned into his nephew's needs and was doing his best for him.

Right now, though, he was pouring coffee for her, and she acknowledged him with a soft 'Thanks' as he pushed the cup towards her.

'That's good,' she told Harry. 'I heard that you had started school. Are you getting on all right there?'

Harry shrugged. 'It's OK,' he said, losing interest. 'I thought my mum would take me there every day. I don't like it without my mum.' His upper lip jutted a little and she guessed he was doing his best not to cry.

'It's hard for you, isn't it?' Megan's heart went out to the vulnerable child. 'I'm sure your mother wanted to be able to stay with you and look after you, though. I expect she would love to know that you've settled in all right at school, and it would make her happy if you made some new friends there.'

He didn't seem to be paying any attention to what she was

saying, and she could only begin to imagine how the boy was feeling. He was so young, and his relationship with his mother must have meant everything to him.

She had no idea what that was like, to have a parent who was her whole world.

Things had been so different for her after all. She had been older when her mother had left the family home, just starting out at secondary school, and all she could recall was the sense of utter shock and despair when she'd realised that she had gone. She remembered being overcome by a feeling that she must have done something wrong and therefore she wasn't worthy of having her mother stay around. Why else would she have gone away?

Harry for the most part seemed to keep his emotions locked inside himself. His face had taken on a closed expression, but after a second or two he put down his sandwich and started to make 'brumming' noises with his car once more.

'Have a seat,' Theo said, pulling out a chair for her at the table. He was looking at her with an odd expression, as though he was trying to work out what was going through her mind.

Megan glanced at him in return and then looked away, sitting down as he'd suggested. Perhaps that was what set him apart from others. He was more perceptive than most, and it was clear that he cared about people.

'I made a selection of sandwiches, so you can have whatever you like—cheese, salad, ham or chicken.' He slid the platter towards her and handed her a plate. 'There's some hot vegetable soup as well, if you'd like some.'

'I thought something in here smelt really appetising.' She sniffed the air appreciatively. Her grey eyes held a rueful glimmer as she glanced across the table at him. 'At this rate, I'm going to owe you a meal or two.'

His mouth tilted at the corners. 'It's the least I can do, since you're here to help me out. And from the sound of it, you've been working all day, too. You need sustenance.'

He ladled soup from a plain glazed tureen into a bowl and passed it to her. 'You said you had been out with the ambulance,' he murmured, sitting opposite her and helping himself to soup. 'Is that part of your work with the hospital?'

'It's more of a voluntary role at the moment, though we…John and I…are holding talks with the hospital trust board to see if we can make the work contract based.' She tasted the soup, savouring it for a moment on her tongue before swallowing. 'This is delicious,' she told him, and then went on to add, 'As it is right now, I give up some of my free time so that I can be on call with the ambulance service.'

He frowned. 'Doesn't that make life difficult for you? It can't leave you with much spare time. I know I said you were always busy, but that's taking things to the extreme, isn't it?'

'Not really. I'm glad to do it because I feel that it's really worthwhile. It's only necessary for me to go out with them if the cases are particularly serious and they would benefit from having a doctor on board.'

'And that's what happened today?'

'Yes. I was called out because a man fell from a ladder and had a particularly bad head injury, among other things. There was no ambulance available immediately, so I was asked to go to him as a first responder, along with the local GP. We worked with him for over an hour, tending to his injuries. I had to anaesthetise him and put him on a ventilator to help him breathe—procedures which, as you probably know, paramedics aren't allowed to do. As emergency on-call doctors we carry with us some specialised types of equipment that aren't found on board ambulances.'

'So I guess your actions would have saved his life. He would probably not have survived the journey to hospital otherwise.' He frowned. 'How's he doing?'

She gave a grimace. 'He's as well as can be expected after everything that happened to him. At least we managed to stabilise his condition temporarily. We'll know more in a few days.'

'Hmm. How are your other patients doing—the ones I know about, that is…the man from the pub, the woman who went into cardiogenic shock and the woman who suffered from the pulmonary embolism? Have you had any follow-up information on any of them?'

The fact that he had asked made her warm to him even more. They weren't just sick people to him—he really cared about what happened to them. 'The man from the pub had a benign tumour that was causing his symptoms. It was removed, and he's recovering well. Last I heard, they were all doing fine.' She smiled. 'Knowing that is what makes the job worthwhile.'

'I suppose it does.' He frowned. 'I wouldn't know, really… I seem to have been caught out by the downside of medicine of late.'

'Oh, but it isn't all like that,' she said quickly, feeling a sudden stab of concern for him. His expression was bleak, and it brought home to her that she had no experience of the torment he had been going through these last few months. Surely it couldn't bode well for him if he were to stay away from his profession for too long? The more he avoided facing up to the situations that haunted him, the less chance he would have of ever becoming whole again.

She reached out and touched his hand momentarily, a searing contact that brought his gaze to meet hers fully and made her realise how much she wanted to offer him comfort.

'There are good times,' she murmured, 'as we've just seen, exhilarating moments when you know that you've made a difference. Perhaps you've been unfortunate in your experiences, but you're a highly skilled surgeon, and if you aren't there to help out, people will suffer as a result.' She frowned. 'That's why we would dearly like to have you work with us at the hospital.'

She paused to take a quick breath, and when he didn't comment on what she had said, she ploughed on. 'Would you not consider going back to work, even on a part-time basis? That would still give you time to care for Harry and allow you to look in on his mother every day.' She glanced at the boy to see if he was listening in on their conversation, but the child was engrossed in his game.

'The ambulance work that I'm involved with might be right up your street,' she tacked on, warming to her theme, 'and I would so love to involve other people in setting up a new system. I'm positive that we could save so many lives by developing a service where skilled emergency doctors attend to the patient on site.'

'This is your pet project, isn't it? I can see how enthusiastic you are about it,' he teased.

She nodded. 'Yes, I am, that's true… But it could work for you, too, I'm sure of it.' She studied him intently for a second or two, before adding, 'Surgery is such a specialised branch of medicine, where you have little actual day-to-day contact with people as ordinary human beings. Instead, they are anaesthetised and remote, and surgery is a kind of mechanical skill, isn't it, where you fix them and put things right?'

She broke off and made an odd little gesture with her hands as though to emphasise her point. 'I mean, the change of pace might be just what you need to get you back into doing what you're best at—being a doctor, dealing with people who might relate to you in a different way.'

He shook his head, a frown indenting his brow. 'I have too many other concerns right now. I'm needed here.'

It was an excuse, she was sure of it, and her heart ached for him. It was easy to understand the way he must be feeling, the wariness, the inability to take that step forward into the abyss, hence the guarded reaction he was giving her.

She said softly, 'I expect we could sort something out with the hospital management so that you could be employed on a short-term contract to see if it suited you.' She was pretty certain that John would move heaven and earth to devise a contract that would allow them to bring Theo on board. 'And, as I said, you might even want to try working on a part-time basis, with hours to suit yourself.'

She tried to gauge Theo's reaction to what she was saying, but his expression was noncommittal for the most part, and she decided to take that as a vaguely positive sign. 'It wouldn't be what you were used to, of course, but you would be doing valuable work with critically ill patients all the same. There wouldn't be the same burden of pressure that you had in Theatre because you would be treating patients from the outset and what happens to them after that would depend equally on other members of the team.'

She watched the expressions flickering across his face, uncertain whether her plea had fallen on stony ground.

His shoulders moved in a dismissive fashion. 'And as I said to you before, I don't have any plans to go back to medicine. I'm making a comfortable enough living from my investments so I don't have any material need to go back to work. I can manage well enough with the rental income from my property.'

The breath slowly left her lungs. She had failed again. 'I shouldn't have brought it up,' she said softly, reluctantly acknowledging defeat. 'It just seemed to me that you would be ideal for the job and perhaps the job was what you needed too, but I can see that you've made up your mind. I won't mention it again.'

She leaned back in her seat, trying to come to terms with the finality of the situation. Then, after a moment or two, she broke off a piece of crusty bread and tasted it. 'This food is wonderful,' she told him, making an effort to change the subject. 'Everything is so fresh and wholesome. I could get used to it. I can't say that I relish going home and having to cook something for myself each evening, and I certainly couldn't come up with anything as mouth-watering as this soup.'

'I've always enjoyed home-made soups. I watched my mother at work in the kitchen when I was young, and she was a sure hand at cooking, so much so that I've gained an interest in it to some extent. At my place in Somerset I grow vegetables and herbs in my garden to use in various recipes, but what you're eating now is produce from the local market... onions, carrots, peas and lentils combined with stock. It's easy enough to prepare and doesn't take too long to cook, and added to that it gives Harry a lot of the nutrients he needs.' He gave a wry smile. 'As you see, I have plenty of time on my hands.'

'And you're making good use of it, taking care of your nephew.' She respected him for that, for the way he had taken the boy in and was doing his best to smooth the way for him.

She sent him a brief glance. 'Of course, it most likely means that you'll also have time to start working on the house. I've managed to come up with one or two ideas for your furnishings if you want to hear them.'

He nodded. 'Shall we go through the rooms one by one, whenever you're ready?'

'If you like.' She swallowed the last of her coffee and wiped her hands on a serviette. 'I'm ready now.'

'Good.' He stood up and went over to Harry. 'If you've finished eating, you could go and play with your toys in the other room.' He glanced at his watch. 'There's still half an hour left before bedtime.'

'OK.' Harry slid down from his seat, taking time to set his car in motion as he headed towards the adjoining reception room.

'Actually, that was the first room I had in mind,' Megan said, following the boy's progress with her gaze. 'It occurred to me that if you wanted to do something on a bigger scale, you could knock through the wide alcove in this wall to form an archway and open it up into the reception room.'

She tried to show him with the sweeping gesture of her arm where the arch could be formed. 'Then you would have a dining room adjoining the kitchen, and some of the furniture—the wooden dresser and the oak dining table and chairs—could be brought in from the other reception room. They would look much better in there, and you have the added interest of French doors leading out onto the terrace. It would make it a delightful room to eat in, with the view of the garden. I know you already have a small table and chairs in the kitchen, but a dining room close by would be useful.'

They walked into the room in question and her mouth quirked as she gazed out of the French doors at the distant shrubbery and the trellised arch covered by scrambling clematis that was just coming into bloom. 'You even have a bird table outside on the lawn. I imagine it would be lovely to sit at your leisure and watch the birds feeding out there.'

He appeared to be thinking things through, all the while

looking around. 'Yes,' he said after a moment or two. 'You're right. I don't know why I didn't think of it before. It makes perfect sense.'

'Unless you didn't want to go to the trouble of taking out part of the wall? You've only just had the kitchen remodelled, haven't you? It would mean making some changes that perhaps you aren't keen on.'

He stared about him once more. 'That was done a while ago. Actually, what you're suggesting wouldn't take much of an effort, and it won't cause any structural problems. There's already a supporting beam in place, and that part of the kitchen lends itself to extension. It would only mean that we lose the place where the Welsh dresser is standing, and that could just as easily go into the dining room.' He turned to her, throwing her that crooked grin of his. 'You're a genius. I knew I was doing the right thing, asking you to come over here to take a look.'

'I'm glad to be of service,' she said, her tone light. 'As to the other rooms, I thought maybe you could turn the smaller bedroom into a study.'

They walked back into the kitchen, and she went on with her outline. 'There are bookcases that could go up there, along with the writing desk and bureau and a couple of armchairs. Add a cosy rug and it would be a wonderful room to work in. Of course, if you wanted to keep it as a guest bedroom, you might want to add a sofa bed instead of the armchairs.'

He slid his arm around her waist and gave her a hug, so that a thrill of warmth swept through her. 'You're amazing. It's such a simple solution, and it must have been staring me in the face the whole time, yet I missed it.' His hand came to rest on the curve of her hip, evoking warm ripples of sensation that eddied and flowed like the tide. 'I can't imagine what I'm going to do without you to guide me through the make-over in the next few months. You wouldn't care to stay on here and be my mentor, would you? I promise I'll feed you and relieve you of all cooking chores for the foreseeable future.'

'That's a very tempting offer…but the answer is, no, thank you, absolutely not.' She was laughing at him, but all the time she was conscious of that strong male arm around her waist, tugging her close to him. He was warm and virile and every nerve ending in her body was feverishly aware of him and clamouring for more.

She loved the intimacy of that embrace, yet deep down she was afraid of what the consequences might be if she gave in to her wilder feelings and snuggled up against him as the arms wrapped around her were coaxing her to do.

Nothing good would come of it, that was for sure. Life simply didn't go that way for her.

'Are you certain?' He was gazing down at her, amusement dancing in his blue eyes, and her resolve almost melted away in that instant as her gaze meshed with his.

'Quite sure,' she said on a breathless note, her heart pounding against her rib cage. 'You see, I know your type. You entice people here under false pretences and then try to charm them into doing your will.' She treated him to a smoke-grey stare. 'I'm made of sterner stuff than that, hadn't you realised?'

He shook his head, not letting her go. Instead, he drew her even closer so that her hip was crushed against his and the softness of her breasts melded with the hard wall of his chest. 'That's a shame,' he said with a wicked grin. 'I thought I might lure you up to my garret and persuade you to pose for me. There's nothing I'd like more than to capture you on canvas.'

'See what I mean?' Laughter gurgled in her throat, while all the time her body reacted in tingling response to the way his hard, muscled torso was pressed up against her and every fibre of her being was catapulted into vibrant life. 'You're irrepressible,' she said huskily. 'And with a child under your roof, too.'

'Ah, yes, my young nephew,' he murmured. 'That reminds me of how near it is to his bedtime.' Slowly, he began to release her. 'Just give me a moment or two and the situation will be remedied in a flash. I'll be back before too long, and we can take up where we left off.'

'Don't rush on my account,' she said, coming gradually down to earth once more as their bodies drew apart. 'Harry needs you. I'll take the time to clear away the supper dishes.'

'You don't have to do that.' He had sobered now, and was eyeing her thoughtfully. 'Joking apart, I'm really grateful to you for your advice, you know. Sit down and help yourself to more coffee while I go and see to the lad. I'd like to go through your ideas with you. Maybe we could work on some changes to the décor while we're about it. I had it in mind to freshen up the walls and my mother thought the place could do with new curtains. I just don't know what sort of thing to choose.'

Megan's heart rate juddered into a more even beat. She was right not to have taken him seriously. He was teasing her, having a bit of light-hearted fun, that was all, and she was doing the sensible thing in trying to keep a safe distance from him.

'This is more than just a temporary makeover, then?' she managed. 'I thought you mentioned that you might go back to Somerset at some point?'

His eyes took on a distant look. 'That's true enough, though I do have several options to think about. I was offered a position overseas—it would involve less hands-on surgery and allow me to take on a teaching role, but I can't bring myself to dwell on either right now. As things are, I prefer to take one day at a time, and I may as well be comfortable while I'm doing that.'

'That's understandable, I suppose.' She was still trying to take in what he had said. He had been offered a position overseas? She hadn't been expecting that, and her world seemed to have dimmed all at once, because in these last couple of days she had come to enjoy being with him, and had even found herself looking forward to seeing more of him.

He went off in search of Harry and Megan turned her attention to clearing the table. It helped to have something to do, to take her mind off what he had said.

The disappointment stayed with her. It dawned on her that she had noticed so many things about him…the way he smiled, and even a brief quirk of his mouth seemed to brighten up the room and make it seem as though all was fresh and new.

How had it happened that he had managed to get under her skin? He had cooked for her, invited her to share in the warmth and comfort of his family home, to witness the bond of affection between him and his young nephew. There were so many things that she would miss if he were to leave.

It was all too unsettling, and she concentrated her attention instead on loading the dishwasher and wiping down the surfaces with a soft cloth. There was a certain amount of distraction to be had, she discovered, in restoring the beautiful kitchen to its pristine glory.

The phone rang as she was draping the tea-towel over the rail on the range cooker and she paused for a moment, wondering whether she ought to answer it for Theo if he was busy. The ring tone cut off after a moment or two, though, and she guessed he must have used an extension in the bedroom.

He came downstairs some five minutes later, and she could

see straight away that something was wrong. His features were drawn, his expression preoccupied.

'Was it the phone call?' she asked. 'Have you had bad news?'

'I have to go to the hospital,' he said. 'They say Francie has taken a turn for the worse and I need to go to her. Apparently she was asking for me.' He frowned. 'I should call my mother and ask if she'll come over to look after Harry.' He glanced at her. 'Would you mind very much waiting with him until she gets here?'

'I'll stay and watch him for you,' she said quickly. 'There's no need to disturb your mother unless you want to.'

He grimaced. 'I was a little worried about that, I'll admit. She's bound to be upset, and I don't want to alarm my parents unnecessarily. I'd sooner find out exactly what the situation is before I talk to them.'

'Then you should take me up on my offer. Is Harry in bed?'

'He's tucked in and already half-asleep.' His frown deepened. 'Are you sure you don't mind staying on here?'

'I'll be happy to look after him,' she answered. 'Does he have any idea of what's happening?'

He shook his head. 'None at all. I've told him that I have to go out, but that he won't be left on his own and I'll be back as soon as I'm able.'

'And is he OK with that?'

'He seems to be. He's very tired. School seems to be affecting him that way.'

'OK. You go, then. I'll make sure that he's all right. You won't need to worry about him.'

He hesitated, a muscle flicking in his jaw as though he was being torn apart by some silent enemy, and she could readily sympathise with his predicament. His sister was in danger and her son was vulnerable. Theo was fighting against all odds, doing what he could to keep up a semblance of normality. She wanted to reach out to him and offer him what solace she could.

'Don't worry about hurrying back,' she told him. 'I'll stay as long as is necessary.'

'Thanks.' He looked at her with relief in his eyes and she reached out to him and held him close for a moment or two. His arms came around her in return and she felt the tension locked in his bunched muscles for an instant before he moved away from her and hurried out of the house.

After he had gone, it seemed to Megan that the light had gone out of the place without his vital, energetic presence. She could only hope that his sister would rally, for all their sakes.

CHAPTER SIX

THE house was silent after Theo left, and for a while Megan felt a strange sense of isolation, as though all the warmth had seeped out of her life.

She tried to shake off the feeling, and went upstairs to look in on Harry. He was in the room next to Theo's, snuggled down beneath a cosy duvet, and for a while she watched the sleeping child and wondered how he would cope with the knowledge that his mother had taken a turn for the worse. If only she and Theo could have protected him from that...but, of course, it was out of their hands. She wished that she could help him in some way.

Glancing around the shadowed room, she guessed that Theo had gone to some trouble to make sure that his young nephew would feel at home here. The theme was blue-grey with hints of gold, with the colours reflected in the duvet and the curtains, along with a racing-car design.

It was decorated with a young boy in mind, and there was everything in here that the child could want. There were colourful books on the shelves, toys that she guessed had been brought from his home and a soft carpet underfoot where he could sit and play. Apart from the kitchen that had been thoroughly upgraded, it seemed as though Theo had concentrated on doing up this room and his own bedroom as priorities.

The boy stirred, mumbling in his sleep, as though he was in the middle of a troubled dream, and she waited for a few minutes until he settled down once more. Then she crept quietly out of the room and made her way downstairs.

What had happened to Theo's sister? Had she suffered another bleed inside her head? Theo hadn't said anything about what was going on, other than that the hospital was concerned. He had been naturally anxious to get to her as quickly as possible.

Megan glanced at the clock on the wall of the kitchen. It was already past midnight and there had been no word from him, no phone call or text message to say what was going on. Did that signify good news or bad?

She went into the living room and sat down to read the newspaper for a while, more to take her mind off the events of the day than anything else. She switched on the lamp by her armchair, and tried to concentrate on the articles, letting her gaze wander from time to time to the beautiful old fireplace where orange and gold flames flickered in the grate and cast warm pools of light around the room. Was this where Theo sat of an evening, thinking about his family and his troubled life back in Somerset? Would he really leave all this and go back there one day? Sadness washed over her at the thought.

Some time later she became aware of a faint noise that disturbed her reading. The sound seemed to be coming from upstairs, and she stood up and hurried out into the hallway. Had Harry woken up?

There were muffled cries coming from his room, and she started up the stairs, wondering what might have woken him. As she drew nearer to the landing, she realised that the child was calling out, muttering broken words and part-formed sentences as though he was still half-asleep.

'No, no... Want to go there... You take me...'

Megan opened the door to the boy's bedroom and stepped quietly into the room. Harry was lying on the bed, the duvet in a tangled heap around his legs. His hair was tousled and a faint sheen of sweat beaded his brow. His eyes were open and he stared at her, his gaze filled with confusion and distress.

'It's all right, Harry,' she murmured, going over to him. 'I think you must have been having a bad dream.' She sat down carefully on the side of his bed, gently straightening the duvet and lightly stroking his hair.

'They were going without me,' he said in a thready voice.

'Who was going without you?'

'Everybody. They were getting on the bus and they left me behind.'

'It was just a dream,' she said again. 'Nobody's leaving you. You're safe.'

He gulped in a breath. 'I want my mum.' His voice choked in his throat. 'I want my mum to come and see me.'

'I know you do, Harry.' She reached in the pocket of her jeans for a clean tissue and tenderly wiped the dampness from his brow. His face was flushed, and she added in a quiet tone, 'Would you like me to get you something to drink?'

'No. I want my mum. I want Uncle Theo.'

'He'll come and see you soon. You'll be able to talk to him and tell him all about it.' She sought for ways to divert his attention and help him calm down. 'In the morning you'll be able to show him how fast your racing car can go, won't you? I saw that you were playing some good games with it earlier. Were you driving it along a racetrack?'

'I want Uncle Theo.' Tears streaked the child's cheeks, and

Megan realised that nothing she said was doing any good. He was still upset, still moving restlessly in the bed, tossing his head from side to side.

'Where is he?' Harry cried. 'Why isn't he here?' He moved suddenly, brushing her arm away from him as he turned his head into his pillow and began to sob afresh.

Megan looked at him and tried to hide the despair she was feeling. He wanted nothing to do with her, and she didn't have any idea how she was going to be able to calm him down. She was a relative stranger to him, and she didn't know the first thing about the special bond between a mother and child. She had never experienced it first hand and all she had to call on was the tug of emotion she felt whenever she looked at this troubled boy.

'He had to go out for a little while,' she murmured, 'but I'm sure he'll be back before too long.' She hoped that was true.

'Will he?' Harry looked up at her doubtfully. 'Will you ask him to come up and see me when he gets back?'

She nodded. 'If that's what you want...but you might be asleep by then.'

'Tell him to wake me up. Promise me you'll ask him to come and talk to me?'

'All right. I promise.' She glanced around at the nearby bookshelf. 'Would you like me to read you a story from one of your books to help settle you down?'

He shook his head. 'My mum reads me stories. You're not my mum.' His face crumpled again and Megan reached for him and gathered his resisting body into her arms, holding him close. She kissed his temple and stroked his head, doing whatever she could to comfort him.

'I know,' she said. 'I know. I'm sorry.'

He sobbed against her breast, and after a while the sobs

turned to little hiccups, gradually dwindling away. He relaxed against her finally and she held him, cradling him in her arms until the sound of his breathing told her that he had fallen asleep at last.

Some time later she laid him gently down so that his head rested on the pillow, and she covered his shoulders once more with the duvet.

She sat with him for a few more minutes, until she was sure that his breathing was slow and even, and then she stood up and quietly left the room.

Downstairs, in the kitchen, she switched on the kettle and made herself a hot drink. Her emotions were churned up inside her, and she needed time to gather herself together.

Theo's key turned in the lock as she was about to go into the living room a few minutes later, and she caught her breath in expectation. How would he be feeling? Was his sister out of danger? She found herself waiting, hoping for his sake that all was well. She stood still and watched him come into the hallway, all the time guardedly watching his expression.

'You're still up,' he said, his voice edged with weariness as he shut the door behind him. 'I imagined that you would be curled up on the sofa by now, fast asleep.'

She shook her head. 'I was concerned about what was happening with your sister. Besides, Harry woke up. He had a bad dream and he was very upset.'

'Was he?' Theo winced. 'I'll go up and check on him in a minute or two.'

She nodded. 'He's asleep now, but he was asking for you...and for his mother. I had to promise you'd wake him when you got back. He needs the reassurance that you're here, I think.' She wanted to ask him how his visit to the hospital had gone, but she thought better of it, giving him time to get himself together.

His mouth flattened. 'He does that. He's become quite clingy these last few weeks and he's had several disturbed nights. There's no school tomorrow, so at least he can have a lie-in in the morning.' He grimaced. 'None of this has been easy for him, and I don't suppose it helped very much, bringing him here to unfamiliar surroundings—though he has visited this house with his mother once or twice in the past.'

They walked towards the kitchen. 'The water in the kettle is hot,' Megan said. 'I could make you a drink, if you like.'

He nodded. 'Thanks. I'd like that.' He went to stand by the range and leaned against the handrail as though he was still trying to come to terms with all that was going on.

'How is Francie?' Megan asked, pulling in a deep breath to prepare herself for his answer as she flicked the switch on the kettle and took a mug from the shelf. 'Have there been any new developments?'

His blue eyes clouded. 'She has pneumonia. I think the infection must have been coming on over the last few days. When she first had the brain haemorrhage it left her unable to swallow, and the doctors think she might have inhaled something into her lungs. It could have been food, liquid or vomit, but it led to an infection in her lungs.'

Megan was alarmed by that news. Pneumonia was a bad complication, coming on top of everything else that Francie had suffered. It was a symptom that could affect her chances of recovery, and might even prove fatal.

'I'm so sorry. That's the last thing she needed after all that's happened. What are they doing to treat her?'

'They took her up to the bronchoscopy suite. The consultant did his best to try to suck out whatever it was in her lungs that had caused the problem in the first place. He did it while I was there this evening, and now they have her on strong anti-biotics. All we can do is wait and see how she responds.'

Megan rested a hand lightly on his arm, wanting to offer what comfort she could. 'I'm sorry you're having to go through this. It must be really hard for you.'

'I didn't know it was possible to feel so helpless.' He drew in a shuddery breath. 'She's my only sister and I love her dearly. We used to bicker all the time when we were young-sters, but we were always good friends, no matter what. I used to complain to the boys I went around with that she would follow me everywhere, but I didn't really mind. She had an inquisitive nature, and she wanted to join in with everything. That's what makes this so hard. I can't bear to see her like this, so weak and unable to do anything for herself.'

He turned to face her and she moved closer to him and gave him a hug, wanting to take some of the burden from him in any way she could. She didn't know why she felt this way, only that she could empathise with his struggle, and she hated to think that he was going through it alone. She would do whatever she could to help him through this.

'I'm glad that you're here with me,' he said softly, return-ing the embrace and dropping a light kiss on the top of her head.

It was a natural gesture, a quick reaction to her offer of comfort, but the sensation of his arms going around her and the gentle touch of his lips on her hair made the blood pulse through her veins in a flood of heat. It felt good to be close to him this way.

'I should go and look in on Harry,' he said a moment or two later, slowly releasing her and putting some space between them.

'Yes, of course.' She was out of synch with everything for

a moment, at a loss to know what to do. 'I suppose I ought to go home. I've intruded on you for long enough.'

He frowned. 'It's very late for you to be driving, and you must be tired by now after such a long day. Why don't you stay over? Do you have to work in the morning?'

She shook her head. 'No. It's my day off.'

'Well, then, there's no problem. I can put fresh linen on the bed in the guest room, if you like. I'm sure I have a spare toothbrush in the bathroom cabinet, and there's a new night-dress and towelling robe that I bought for my sister in a bag somewhere. I meant to take them to the hospital for her today, but it slipped my mind.'

His suggestion had taken her by surprise. 'Are you sure?' The thought of driving anywhere at this late hour wasn't appealing, but the idea that she might stay there hadn't occurred to her.

'I'm positive.' He made a face. 'It's been good to have you here. All this has been a real eye-opener for me, you know. I'm used to making the rules as I go along, acting in a decisive manner most of the time, but since Francie was taken ill, everything has gone out of the window. Living here with Harry has thrown my whole world out of kilter. I'm just not used to being a surrogate father. Francie was the one who always knew what to do. She was great with him, but I'm dealing with the unknown, feeling my way an inch at a time, and it's more difficult than anything I've ever had to deal with.'

'You're short-changing yourself,' Megan said, holding out a mug of hot tea to him. He had no idea just how well he was doing, and she was determined to bolster him. 'You must be doing a great job, because you've helped the boy to cope with all the changes he's had to endure over these last few weeks. Harry thinks the world of you. He was asking for you, and no one else would do, except for his mother.'

She pressed her lips together as though that would in some way help take away the discomfort that suddenly swamped her. 'I didn't know how to soothe him after his bad dream. I tried…I talked to him, I thought I might manage to distract him, but I didn't even begin to make first base. He only wanted you. In the end I held him close and he fell asleep in my arms, but it just brought it home to me that I'd never be any good as a parent. I had this churned-up feeling inside, and I felt so helpless. I realised that I don't know the first thing about relating to young children.'

'Why are you being so hard on yourself? It sounds as though you followed your instincts, which is what we all do in the end. You did the right thing in holding him. We may not know how to handle every situation, but we all have the urge to love and comfort one another.' He drank from the mug. 'Isn't that something we all learn from the bond we have with our parents?'

She gave a light shrug. 'I wouldn't know about that. I never had that kind of relationship with mine.'

He frowned. 'I don't think I follow you. Are you saying that your mother wasn't a caring sort of person?'

She shook her head. 'Not that I recall. She was always too busy with her own interests to take any notice of what was going on around her. There were lots of rows between her and my father, and I had the feeling that I was in the way most of the time.'

'There must have been occasions when she was affectionate towards you?'

'Possibly, but I suspect that they were few and far between. Anyway, when I was eleven she walked out of the family home and never came back.'

Theo stared at her. 'You're not serious?'

'I am.'

'Did she tell you that she was going?'

'I don't think so.' She thought about it for a moment, her brows meeting in a crooked line. 'She just went out of the door one day and disappeared from our lives. She may have said something to my father beforehand about leaving, but he didn't seem to accept that she meant it. He said she would come back at some point and if that happened he'd send her on her way again.'

'But she didn't?'

'No.' Megan sighed. 'At first I was worried sick that she might come home and he would throw her out before I had the chance to talk to her. I pleaded with him, but he was angry and wound up over the things that had gone wrong between them and he wasn't really listening to me. So I started to make all sorts of different plans so that if she did turn up he wouldn't be able to ruin things.'

'Surely she must have sent cards or letters from time to time?'

She nodded. 'At first there would occasionally be a postcard from some seaside town or other, or even a birthday card, but they stopped after a few years. I was hungry for any kind of word from her. I would wait for the postman, longing for a letter from her, a note, anything to show that she had been thinking about us, but they hardly ever came. I couldn't believe that she had gone for good. It wore me out emotionally, waiting for her, and it took me a long time to realise that I was living a fantasy where my mother loved me and was going to come back.'

She gave a shuddery sigh. 'I had been kidding myself all along. Eventually I realised that she didn't want to know, that she only ever really thought about herself and what would make her happy. I was in the way, something she could do without.'

Theo put down his mug and came over to her, drawing her to him. 'I had no idea that you had been through something like that. I can't get my head round what it must be like to have your mother turn away from you. You must have been through hell and back.'

She rested her head against his chest, reassured by the rhythm of his heart, beating steadily beneath her cheek. 'It was a shock, to begin with,' she murmured. 'Then I was numb, and couldn't work out what I had done wrong to make her want to leave. I tried being good, tidying my room, working hard at school. I thought somehow she might find out that I was worthy of being her daughter after all.'

'Poor angel,' he murmured, wrapping his arms around her and holding her close. 'I can't begin to imagine what that must have been like for you.'

'I got over it a long time ago,' she said, loving the way his hands caressed her, stroking the length of her spine, drawing her into the shelter of his strong, powerful body. He was her protection against the storm, against the ravages of life itself.

'I'm not so sure that's true,' he said softly. 'How can anyone ever get over something like that?'

'You learn to take one day at a time, and you fill your hours with work so that you can take consolation in what you do. I feel that I'm helping people through my work, so it makes up for what happened in the past and it gives me a feeling of self-worth.' She looked up at him with sudden remorse in her gaze. 'I don't know why I'm telling you all this. You have enough problems to contend with. You must be worried sick about your sister, and yet you've let me run off at the mouth all this time about my own problems.'

'I'm glad that you felt able to confide in me.' His glance trailed over her, his expression tinged with sadness. 'It's true that I'm concerned about Francie. It's frustrating, not being able to do anything to help her. She was fretting about Harry, and all I could do was to promise her that I'll take care of him.'

Absently, he ran his hands through the silky length of her hair, his thumb brushing the softness of her cheek. 'Somehow I'll have to find a way of explaining things to my parents. They were hoping that she was on the mend.'

'Is there any sign that the antibiotics are working?'

He shook his head. 'Not as yet. I guess it will be a few days before we know anything for sure.' His mouth straightened. 'I'd better go up and see Harry.' He braced himself for action. 'Then I'll make the bed up for you in the guest room.'

She eased herself away from him. 'I'll do that if you tell me where things are. You go and talk to Harry. Take your time.'

A short while later Megan finished smoothing the duvet on the bed in her room. She gathered up the nightdress and robe that Theo had put out for her, tracing her fingers over where he must have held them. She laid the bundle lightly against her cheek for a moment or two before straightening and crossing the corridor to the guest bathroom.

Harry's bedroom door was open, and as she passed by she could see that Theo was quietly talking to the child and Harry appeared to be content. Whatever Theo said about not knowing how to handle the situation, he was working wonders. He was being guided by his instincts, and they didn't appear to be letting him down.

He would make a wonderful father. Harry wasn't his child, but she knew with certainty that if ever Theo had children of his own he would love and protect them with everything he had. Knowing that made her warm to him all the more.

She went into the bathroom to prepare for bed. It had been a long, long day, and somehow her whole world seemed to have changed. Was it possible that she was falling for Theo? How else could she account for this tide of warm feeling that was sweeping over her?

But it wasn't to be, was it? Theo was working his way through a quandary of his own and was in no fit state to be accountable for his emotions where she was concerned. He may feel gratitude towards her, thankfulness for her companionship in his hour of need, but that was as far as his feelings might extend.

And as for Megan, no matter how much she was growing to care for him, she knew that her instincts were not to be trusted. She had learned all too harsh a lesson in the past that those she loved would not stay around for long enough to return her feelings, and the only result to emerge from her dreams would be a badly trampled heart.

How could she bear it if she was to let herself love him and he didn't return those feelings?

CHAPTER SEVEN

'CAN we have a puppy, Uncle Theo? Timmy at school has one—He says it's a sort of spangle dog, and they call him Sniffer because he always has his nose into everything. I really, really want a puppy. Can we, please?'

Megan was just emerging from the bedroom, still wearing her nightclothes and yawning sleepily as she readied herself to face the new day, when she heard Harry's voice. The sound was coming from his bedroom, and as she made her way towards the guest bathroom she saw that his door was open. Theo, already fully dressed, was helping him to sort out the clothes that he was going to wear that day.

'A puppy?' Theo echoed, a note of complete surprise in his voice, making Megan smile. How on earth was he going to get out of that one? 'I don't think I've ever heard of a spangle puppy,' he murmured. 'Do you mean spaniel?'

She guessed he was playing for time. Pushing open the door to the bathroom, she heard Harry's reply.

'Spaniel, yes, that's it. He's gorgeous. All brown and white, with long curly ears.'

'He sounds terrific,' Theo said, 'but, you know, puppies are not like toys. They have to be fed and watered and taken for regular walks, and they make lots of messes about the place until they're house-trained. There's lots of cleaning up to be done after them, and I really don't think we could manage to do all that while we have to go to the hospital every day. It would mean that the puppy would be left on his own a lot.'

'We could take him with us,' Harry persisted, undaunted. 'And I could look after him. I'm good at looking after things.'

Megan closed the door of the bathroom, still smiling. Harry had an answer for everything, and a puppy was surely the pinnacle of desire to a child's mind.

She had a quick shower and towelled herself dry before wrapping herself in the soft white robe that Theo had given her. It was still early in the morning, and she hadn't bargained for either of them being up and about as yet. She had forgotten that some youngsters were full of energy from the moment they awoke.

Her hair was wet from the shower, but there was a hairdryer in her room, and it wouldn't take more than a few minutes for her to finish getting ready. Perhaps she could help out by making breakfast for everyone.

Theo came out on to the landing just as she emerged from the bathroom. He was wearing casual trousers that moulded his hips and led her gaze to his long legs before she took herself in hand enough to lift her eyes. His light-coloured shirt looked good against the golden colour of his skin and showed the flat plane of his stomach.

'There you are,' he said. 'I thought you would still be fast asleep.'

She gave a rueful smile. 'I'd planned on getting up first and then I was going to make breakfast for you, but you beat me to it. I heard you talking to Harry earlier.'

His mouth curved briefly. 'I've sent him to get washed and

dressed. I promised him bacon, egg and mushrooms—that always gets him moving.'

'Even more than his longing for a puppy?' Her smile widened, a tender look coming into her grey eyes. 'I heard him badgering you about it.'

'Well, he's hungry, so let's say he's been diverted for a while. Long enough, I hope, for me to be able to come up with a proper answer.' He looked her over, a gleam coming into his eyes. 'You're a sight for sore eyes at this time of the morning, I must say.' His gaze moved over the length of her, taking in the creamy curve of her throat left bare by the robe's wide lapels and shifting downwards to glide along the smooth, lightly tanned expanse of her legs. 'You look fantastic in that robe...' His mouth slanted. 'Though I dare say you'd look even better without it.'

'Oh...' She sucked in a quick breath. Her cheeks flushed with warm colour, and she attempted to draw the robe around her more securely.

'Too late,' he murmured with a chuckle. 'I've already had a glimpse of paradise in those shapely legs. Besides, seeing you every day is enough for me to know that you have a gorgeous body. It would trigger a heart attack in any man with a pulse.'

'You're incorrigible,' she managed, her voice husky with uncertainty. His nearness was having a strange effect on her, making her heart thump wildly against her rib cage and sending her nervous system into chaotic disorder.

'Am I?' His mouth made a crooked shape. 'Actually, you know, I'm coming to realise that I'd really love to paint you. Would you consider posing for me?'

Her eyes widened. He was teasing her, wasn't he? 'Are you serious?'

He nodded. 'Very much so. I'd really like to capture your image on canvas.'

'In your dreams,' she retorted, shaking her head and attempting to pull herself together again. He was simply taking delight in being provocative, wasn't he? 'Anyway, for my part, I'd like you to come and work at the hospital. I think it would be the best thing for you, and get you back on your feet again, but that isn't going to happen, is it?' She confronted him face on, daring him to deny it.

He gave a light shrug. 'You can never be sure…it might.' A half-smile touched his lips. 'Who knows, maybe we could figure out a deal of some sort?'

She stared at him. He had clearly lost his senses, what with the shock of his sister's pneumonia and Harry's sudden request for a puppy.

'You're obviously not yourself,' she murmured. 'You wouldn't be saying this if you were on top of your game.'

'That could well be true,' he agreed. 'I suppose I could put it down to mental meltdown or something. It's all your fault, you know, traipsing about the landing wearing next to nothing. What chance does a man have?'

She sent him an inhibiting glance. 'Don't even go there,' she warned, and started towards her bedroom.

His laughter followed her, echoing in her wake as she pushed her door firmly shut.

His comments had completely thrown her off balance. Of course he didn't mean it. He was teasing her, lightening his load with a moment of fun. He couldn't possibly have been serious, could he?

She dried her hair and then dressed quickly, taking a few minutes to brush her curls until they gleamed. She pinned her hair back with clips and readied herself to go downstairs and face him once more.

'The puppy could play in the garden,' Harry was saying.

'It's a big garden and I could teach it tricks. Timmy's dog knows sit and stay already.' He paused, thinking about that for a moment or two. 'Mind you, he doesn't stay for very long. He keeps getting up and then he goes wandering about.'

'And I expect he chews Timmy's toys, along with the furniture,' Theo said, adding rashers of bacon to the frying pan and adjusting the heat. He turned as Megan walked into the room. 'There's tea in the pot and toast in a rack on the table,' he said, acknowledging her with a smile that made her light up inside. 'Help yourself.'

'Thanks.' She sent him a quick, apologetic glance. 'I really meant to do that for you.'

'It's no problem,' he said. 'Besides, I'm grateful to you for looking after Harry last night, so the least I can do is make breakfast for you. You told me that you don't have to go to work today, didn't you? So you might as well enjoy your leisure time while you can.' He directed a glance towards Harry. 'You should sit yourself down at the table, Harry—the food is ready now.'

Harry did as Theo suggested, and Megan said softly, 'How are you, Harry? Do you think you'll be seeing any of your friends today?'

The child's shoulders lifted in a negligent shrug. 'I don't know. I might be able to go over to Timmy's house for a bit.' He looked across the room at Theo. 'Are we going to see my mum today?'

Theo nodded. 'We'll go to the hospital this afternoon.' He hesitated, pausing in the act of serving out crispy bacon and hash browns. 'She was very poorly yesterday, so she needs to get lots of rest. She couldn't breathe very well, so when you see her you might find that she has an oxygen mask over her face. I don't want you to be alarmed by that.'

Harry frowned. 'How will she be able to breathe with a mask over her face?'

'It's a special one. It helps to give her more air, along with medicine to make her feel better.' Theo slid the plates of food in front of them and then came to sit down at the table.

Megan sent him a quick look. He seemed to be coping well enough after the worry about his sister but, then, she had discovered that he was good at covering his emotions. 'Have you spoken to anyone at the hospital this morning?' she asked.

He nodded. 'They said she had a reasonably comfortable night after the procedure. Her temperature's gone down a little.'

'That's a good sign, isn't it?'

'Yes. It makes me feel a little more optimistic. Though I'll perhaps feel more settled about things when I've been to see her this afternoon.'

He glanced briefly at Harry, and she guessed he was reluctant to linger over the subject in case the boy became upset. He started to eat, and then, after a while, said softly, 'I meant what I said earlier about wanting to paint you. You have a very expressive face, and I'd like to be able to capture just a hint of what I see. It would be a challenge for me to do that.'

'Going back to work would be a bigger challenge, don't you think?' She speared plump mushrooms with her fork, pinioning him with her grey gaze.

She was conscious that she was treading on rocky ground here, but it had somehow become important to her that she did what she could to help him on his way to recovery from the nightmare of what was left of his career.

'You said that you couldn't tackle surgery any more,' she went on, 'but it occurs to me that you need to overcome that hurdle before it becomes a monster. If you leave it too long you'll never go back.'

A muscle contracted in his jaw. 'You have no idea what it's like.'

'Are you quite sure about that? We all have bad experiences at one time or another. As doctors we question whether we're doing everything we can for our patients, or whether we should hone our skills in some way. But mostly we fall back on our professionalism, our training, and know that at least we're doing the best job we can to the utmost of our ability.'

'I tried that. It didn't do me any good. I still felt as though there was lead in the pit of my stomach, and every day turned into a test of endurance. In the end, I couldn't go on.'

She gave him a long look. 'Or maybe you finally gave up because what happened in your private life was that last straw.' She glanced towards Harry, unsure whether or not she should go on.

The boy was engrossed in a complicated procedure of moving beans about his plate, pushing them deliberately into shape with his fork. For a moment she stared at him in puzzlement, uncertain as to what exactly he was doing.

'It looks like a picture of some sort,' Theo said, following her gaze. He frowned, trying to make it out, and then he began to chuckle. 'You need a few more beans on the other end,' he told Harry. 'Do I have it right?' He gestured with his fork over the pattern the boy was making. 'There's the head and the ears, this is the body…and here are the legs. Is there something missing?'

Harry nodded. 'The tail,' he said, moving more beans triumphantly into place. 'See?'

'I do see. Is that what Timmy's puppy looks like?'

Harry studied his creation. 'Well, sort of.' He sent Theo a pleading look. 'Can we have one? Please?'

Theo's expression was guarded. 'I don't think we can look

after one properly just now. How about a guinea pig instead or a baby rabbit? Either of those would be easier to manage.'

Harry's eyes widened. 'Really?'

'It's worth thinking about.'

'I couldn't take a rabbit for a walk.' Harry was frowning now, but there was a thoughtful look about his eyes and clearly he was weighing up the pros and cons.

'Maybe not, but you would be able to play with him on the lawn, and I'm sure we could find plenty of carrots to feed him with. I expect Timmy would like to help you do that.'

Harry took a mouthful of beans and subsided into silence. He was obviously toying with the idea.

'He must have inherited your artistic tendencies,' Megan said, her voice tinged with amusement as she studied the rapidly disappearing bean pool. She sent an oblique glance in Theo's direction. 'It did look quite like a dog, when you think about it.'

Theo made a wry smile. 'Actually, he does like to dabble with paint. He comes with me into the studio and works on his own creations while I daub the canvases.'

She studied him. 'Do you think your painting might have become an escape?'

'From surgery?' He gave the idea some consideration. 'Possibly. I had to find some release from the frustration locked up inside me, and in some ways painting helped to give me that. Perhaps, in my work at the hospital, I wanted to be more than I am. I always aimed to give one hundred per cent, but instead of feeling good about that I had the feeling that something was missing.' He winced. 'It's difficult to explain. I was working to reach the heights of my profession, but there came a time when I felt as though I was wading through heavy water and it was slowing me down, pushing me back when I wanted to go forward.'

Megan frowned. 'You said that you became used to operating on people when it was already too late and little could be done to pull them through, but it doesn't have to be like that, you know. You could do something to remedy that if you really wanted to. If you were to do a stint with the ambulance service as an emergency on-call doctor you might find that you are able to improve your patients' chances of survival from the outset, or maybe you could even help to initiate procedures that would lead to better outcomes for patients.'

'And how would I go about doing that?' His tone showed her that he wasn't convinced but at least this morning he wasn't dismissing the idea out of hand.

'There are research programmes being set up all the time. John has always been keen on raising standards in the emergency department. If you were interested in a project that would help ensure better approaches to care for emergency patients coming into hospital, I'm sure he'd do what he could to help you get started.'

'You mean…something like finding better ways to reduce bleeding after a major injury, or whether carrying out blood tests sooner than normal would help to diagnose a heart attack earlier?'

She nodded. 'That's the sort of thing, yes.'

He stared at her. 'You've been thinking a lot about this, haven't you? Why are you even bothering? You don't actually know anything first hand about the kind of work I used to do, or whether I was any good as a surgeon.'

She arched a brow at him. 'That's not entirely necessary, is it? I've heard so much about what a talented surgeon you are, not just from my boss but also from other colleagues. I've read some of your research papers in the journals, and from being with you I can see that you're a man who cares deeply about the people around you. It seems such a waste for you to give up on surgery altogether when you have such skill.'

'I never said that I'd given up on it altogether. I just needed time and space so that I could think things through.'

'Yes. I realise that.' She hesitated. 'I didn't mean to badger you. It's just that I can't help thinking it would be so much better for you if you could make that leap back into work. Do you mind me talking to you about it?'

He shook his head and his mouth made a wry shape. 'Actually, I think perhaps you're the only one that I can talk to about this in any depth.'

She was touched by that comment. It was good to know that he valued her input, and somehow it brought them closer together.

She queried softly, 'So, have you given it some more thought? Have you managed to come to a decision after all? Will you consider coming to our A and E?'

'Will you reconsider letting me do a portrait of you?'

She looked at him from under her lashes. 'What kind of thing are we talking about?'

His mouth tilted. 'Just a straightforward picture—a head and shoulders study, if you like, or maybe I could show you sitting in a chair by the window. There's a rocking chair up in the studio. You could relax, even read a book. Of course, I'd need to make a few sketches first of all.'

'Oh, I see…I wasn't quite sure…I mean…'

His mouth twisted. 'You thought I wanted to paint you in the nude, didn't you?' Light danced in his eyes as his gaze travelled over her, and Megan felt a wave of heat surge through her, sweeping up to the roots of her hair. 'Well, of course, I would, but since the idea appears to bother you…'

'What's nude?' Harry put in. He appeared to be confused, and was looking intently at Theo.

Theo hesitated for a moment. 'It means without a cover on,' he explained smoothly, keeping his tone even, and Megan lowered her head a fraction and tried not to look at either of them.

'Oh.' Harry was silent for a moment. Then he added, 'I suppose it would be a bit hot up in the studio, especially if the sun's shining. I kick my duvet off sometimes, and Mum says, "Cover yourself up or you might catch cold." But I never do.'

'That's it,' Theo said. 'You have it exactly.'

Megan was relieved when the meal ended. 'If you're going over to the hospital this afternoon,' she said as they cleared the table, 'perhaps I ought to think about taking myself home. There are a few chores I ought to catch up on.'

'You don't have to go,' Theo murmured. 'There are still a few hours left before we need to set off, and I could show you around the village, if you like. We could take a walk by the river. It isn't too far away from here, and the scenery is pretty fantastic. I'm sure Harry would enjoy being out there, and it will help to keep his mind off his mother's illness. He'd be glad of your company.'

Megan wasn't so sure about that. Harry had acknowledged her when she'd asked about his plans for the day earlier, but since then he had said very little to her. Still, the idea of a walk in the countryside was appealing…and the notion that she could spend time with Theo was becoming more and more attractive with every minute that passed.

'I'd like that,' she said. 'I dare say the chores will wait.'

'That's the spirit.' He gave her a crooked smile. 'I'll finish clearing up in here and then get Harry organised.'

They set off some half an hour later to walk along the leafy lane towards the village. The air was warm and fresh, with pale clouds scudding across a misty blue sky, and Megan was relaxed as they walked alongside moss-covered dry stone walls.

Beyond the walls were rocky outcrops, fields covered with meadow flowers, and further on they came across a stream winding its way over a pebble-strewn bed.

At a break in the wall they followed a gravelled track until they came to a stile. Harry was over it in the blink of an eye and they went after him into a lightly wooded area.

'Could we stop here for a while?' he asked, sending Theo an eager glance. 'Is it all right if I climb the trees?'

Theo nodded. 'Go ahead. This one looks easy enough for you to manage. There are lots of low, thick branches. Just don't go too high. Stay where I can reach you.'

They watched as the boy clambered over the branches of a solid ash tree, and Theo slid his arm around Megan's waist and drew her close, stepping back into the shade of an overgrown shrub in order to watch the boy out of the glare of the sun.

'He's like a monkey, heading up into the canopy,' he murmured, his mouth curving. 'It gets so that we can't pass a tree without him wanting to get up there.'

'You have your hands full, that's for sure.' She smiled back at him, and saw the glimmer of mischief that sparked to life in Theo's blue eyes.

'I do, don't I?' He wound his arms around her and tugged her into the warmth of his embrace, bending his head towards her so that his cheek brushed against hers, and in the next moment he sought out her lips and kissed her full on the mouth.

The kiss came as a wake-up call to her entire system. It was a tender, sweet exploration that sent her whole body into a splurge of fizzing excitement. Her mouth softened beneath his, and she clung to him, her head dizzy with overwhelming sensation, her mind clouded with sheer ecstasy as his hands smoothed over her, shaping her curves.

'You're delicious,' he murmured. 'Honey sweet and luscious as a ripe peach.'

His husky words reverberated through her like a lick of flame. She was filled with breathless expectation as he drew her into the shelter of his body. Her soft, feminine contours blended into the muscled wall of his body as though that was exactly where she belonged. Her limbs became weak and insubstantial as if her whole being would meld with his.

'Uncle Theo, I think I'm stuck. I don't know how to get down.' The childish voice brought Megan swiftly back down to earth. It was like a shock wave running through her, and for a second or two she stood perfectly still, letting the torrent flow through her.

Theo slowly eased himself away from her a fraction. 'Stay where you are, Harry,' he said, his gaze lifting to the child. His arm remained around Megan's waist, and she was glad of that, even though his attention was wholly on the boy. She loved this closeness, the feel of his warm body against hers, the way the throb of his heartbeat had pounded against her breast.

After a moment or two he appeared to have worked out what he should do.

'Stay seated and ease yourself sideways along the branch,' he instructed the boy. 'That's it. Take it slowly. There's no rush.' Theo's arm slipped away from Megan, and he began to move towards the child. 'Now, lower your foot on to the branch below. Keep holding on. OK, reach for that overhead branch and steady yourself. Now you can step down. I'll be able to reach you. That's the way.'

Megan stood very still, waiting for the staccato beat of her heart to settle down. He lifted his arms to the boy and took his weight, lowering him to the ground once more. 'So what happened there?' he asked, studying Harry's face. 'How did you manage to get into that scrape?'

'I went too high,' Harry said. 'I know… You told me… But I like going right up as far as I can.'

'You won't like it so much if you fall right down again,' Theo chided, ruffling his hair. 'Come on, monkey legs. It's time we were moving on.'

Megan watched the two of them together. They were a team, with a family bond that held them steadfast, and while it was a joy to witness that special relationship, somehow in that moment she felt utterly out of place.

She didn't belong here, or anywhere. There was no welcoming family unit where she would find her true place. Even her father had left her to herself, being caught up in his own tormented world. It had taught her a harsh lesson. For years now she had been fending for herself, and she had learned to put up a barrier in order to defend herself against the world.

What had she been thinking of, letting Theo kiss her? Didn't she have any sense in her head at all? He was glad to have her around because she was a distraction, someone who took his mind off what was going on in his own life right now. Above all, she had to guard against losing her heart to him.

'Come on, let's go along that path,' Harry was saying. 'Look, there are little holes in the ground over there. What are they?' He looked at Theo for guidance.

'They look like rabbit holes to me,' Theo murmured. 'That's probably where they have their burrows underground.'

'Will we see one? Do they come out?'

'Probably not, while we're close by,' Theo told him.

Megan pulled herself together and went to join them. 'Have you thought about what kind of rabbit you might have for yourself?' she asked the child. 'I saw some lovely lop-eared rabbits at the pet centre when I went to get fish food for the aquarium at the hospital. There were some white ones and some were grey.'

'I don't want a rabbit.' Harry sent her a withering glance. 'I want a puppy. Then I can take him for walks and we can play together.'

'Oh, I see,' she said flatly. 'I didn't know that you had made up your mind against it.'

Harry didn't answer, and she felt the slow wash of dismay run through her. Why was it that she couldn't form any kind of bond with this child?

She was already out of her depth. Life was too full of pitfalls that were ready to swallow her up. Would she never learn that lesson?

CHAPTER EIGHT

'I DON'T know how you managed it, Megan, but you've worked a miracle, it seems.' John was beaming from ear to ear.

Megan looked up from the case notes she was working on and frowned. 'Have I? What miracle would that be? I can't say that I recall anything in particular along those lines.'

'You're too modest by far, my girl.' He waved a sheaf of papers under her nose. 'You know what this is, don't you?'

Megan shook her head. ''Fraid not. You'll have to enlighten me.'

'It's a contract, of course...for Theo Benyon. It's only for a short term, unfortunately, because that's all he would commit to at this point, but it's a start at least.'

Megan's eyes widened. 'You're joking?' She couldn't quite take in what he was saying. Was he really talking about Theo coming there, after all her previous efforts to persuade him had ended in rejection?

'It's no joke, I promise you. It's signed and sealed. I approached him with the offer of a place on our team when he came in to visit his sister a day or so back, and no one was more surprised than I was when he agreed to join us.'

Megan stared at him. 'He's actually agreed to come and work here?'

'Yes, that's right. Only on a part-time basis, mind, because he has too many other responsibilities to deal with just now, but having him accept any kind of position is a great move forward for us. And we have you to thank for it, it seems.'

Her brows lifted. 'Are you sure about that? I thought all my efforts had fallen on stony ground.'

'Not at all. He said he'd been thinking things over after talking to you, and he'd decided that since he could be nearer to his sister by actually working here on the premises, he would accept a short-term contract. We ironed out a deal where he would mostly work with us in A and E, but we added a rota system when he would go along with the ambulance team for a while and provide emergency assistance for the most serious cases, and then follow through with the patients here at the hospital.'

Megan's mouth curved. 'That's great news. You must be very pleased.'

'I am.' He waved the contract about and she guessed that he could hardly contain himself. Then he sobered a little. 'Of course, he has been through a difficult time lately. He told me a little of what was on his mind. He seems to be ready for this on the surface, but it may be that he'll need a lot of support over the coming months.'

It pleased her that John was acknowledging Theo's fears, and that he recognised all was not well with him. Theo managed to put on a cheerful front for the most part, but she sensed that he was covering up his innermost, darkest thoughts, just as he sought diversion in myriad ways. 'Perhaps you shouldn't expect too much of him to begin with,' she said. 'He's been through a lot of late, and with his sister's illness preying on his mind as well it won't be easy for him.'

He frowned. 'That's very true but, then again, we've always

tried to make sure that our staff members have any support that they need.' He gave her a wide smile. 'And that's where you come in, of course. You're just the person he needs to help him through these early days.'

Was she? Megan gave him a wan smile. She wished she could feel as confident in her ability as he obviously did. More than anything, she wanted to help Theo through these difficult times, but Theo was his own man, and she doubted that much of what she had to say made any difference in the long run. Was his decision to come back to work really anything at all to do with what she had said to him? After all, it might have had more to do with his concern for his sister's well-being and wanting to be on hand for her, rather than through any intervention on Megan's part.

Though she had pushed quite hard to convince him that this was the best option for him, hadn't she? It had grieved her to see him wasting his precious skills, and more than that she couldn't help but feel that he was avoiding the issue, using any means of distraction to keep from going back to the profession he had trained for. That must arise from a deep-seated problem at the core of his being and somehow she felt an intense need to shore him up and help him get back on track.

Wasn't she venturing into dangerous waters, though, by doing that? Surely she was heading for a downfall by getting more and more involved with him?

'He'll be in later this morning, ready to start work, after he's dropped young Harry off at school.' John was relishing the moment. 'Stay with him over the next few weeks, and let's give him a full-on Borderlands Hospital welcome. Introduce him to everyone, show him where he can find coffee and snacks throughout the day, and generally make him feel good about being here.' He glanced around. 'Well, I have a meeting up on the third floor, so I'll leave you to it for now. Any problems, be sure to page me.'

'I will.' So the ball was in her court again, was it? Megan thought as she watched her boss walk away. Having Theo working with her on a day-to-day basis promised to be both a blessing and a torment. At the moment, she couldn't work out which one had precedence.

'We have patients coming in from a road traffic accident,' Rhianna announced, cutting in on her thoughts. 'It doesn't look good. There are five casualties, a motorcyclist with head and possible chest injuries and two people with leg trauma. The other two patients are women, one with arm injuries and what looks like whiplash, and the other's a pelvic injury.'

'OK, thanks for that, Rhianna. Sarah will do triage as they come in. We'll keep Resus 1 and 2 clear for them. Theo will be with me and John is at a meeting, but he'll be available if needed. We'd better get the senior house officers on board.'

'I'll page them.' Rhianna hurried away, and Megan slid her case notes into a tray and went to make her preparations. As she came out of the locker room wearing a fresh set of scrubs, she saw Theo coming in through the main doors, his face shadowed and unreadable, though he paused to greet her.

She pulled in a quick breath. How must he be feeling? Surely this must be a momentous, worrying occasion for him, stepping through those doors as a member of a medical team once more? How was he going to cope?

'Theo, I'm really glad to see you here,' she said, going over to him and taking hold of his arm. 'I just heard the news, and I was so surprised when John told me that you had decided to come back to work. I'm overwhelmed that you've actually agreed to do this. It's so good to know that you're going to be working here with us.' She smiled, wanting to show support for him and let him know that she was there for him.

He nodded briefly, a faintly strained expression on his face. 'I must admit I gave it a lot of serious thought.'

'Yes. It can't have been easy for you.' She threw him a penetrating glance. 'What was it that made you change your mind?'

'It was a number of things, I suppose... The fact that by being based here at the hospital I would be able to look in on Francie more often and keep a firm check on her progress.' He hesitated for a second or two. 'Then there was this feeling that I ought to be doing what I could to help people along the road to recovery.' His expression darkened, and she could see that he was still struggling to come to terms with that particular issue.

His tone was edgy. 'It's one thing to have the inherent capacity to do that, but it was slipping away from me day by day. I think I came to realise that I had to prove to myself that I was up to the challenge before it was too late.'

She gave him a quick hug. 'I'm sure you made the right decision, and you know you won't be on your own through any of this. We're all rooting for you, and I'll be here whenever you feel the need to talk.'

His features relaxed momentarily. 'Yes, there was that, too. I don't think I would have chosen to come here if it hadn't been for the fact that I would be able to see you on a daily basis.'

He was looking at her in a curiously intent way and she wasn't quite sure what to make of what he had said. Did he mean that he wanted to be near to her so that he could spend more time with her, or was he simply saying that he would be glad of her support?

Either way, there was no time to dwell on that right now. She was conscious of the wail of sirens in the distance, and her mind was preoccupied with the emergency that was unfolding.

Perhaps her voice betrayed a hint of the pressure she was under. 'Well, as you can hear, you're just in time. We've patients coming in and it looks as though you're very definitely going to be needed. I'll be glad of your help here as soon as you can manage.'

'Yes, I noticed the bustle around Triage as I came in just now. I guessed we were in for a busy morning.'

'You guessed right. There's been a traffic accident. Sorry about the rushed welcome. Perhaps you could find yourself some scrubs from the linen store over there and then come and find me when you're ready? We'll be working in Resus 1 and 2.'

He nodded and she released him, waving a hand in the direction of the room where the uniforms were kept. Her mind was already turning to her patients.

'I'll take the woman with the pelvic injury,' Megan said as Sarah assessed the level of priority amongst the casualties. 'She's unconscious and looks to have come out of this the worst so far. How is the motorcyclist doing?'

'He appears to be stable at the moment. He's able to talk and he seems to know what's going on.'

'All right, then, I think we'll let Theo handle his case.' She moved off with her patient towards Resus 1 just as Theo came forward to receive his patient.

They were working in adjoining bays so as she attempted to stabilise her patient, she could look up from what she was doing and monitor how Theo was coping. He didn't look too good right now. His expression was grim, his shoulders tense, and for a terrible moment she wondered if he was going to be able to get through the day ahead.

His features cleared, though, as he was given the patient's details and approached his bedside. 'How are you feeling, James?' she heard him ask. 'Are you in pain?'

'I'm not too bad, I think,' James answered. He was a young man, around thirty years old, and he explained how he had been thrown off his motorcycle in a high-speed collision with a car. 'I hit something as I landed…I'm not sure what it was. My chest hurts and I've a major headache, but otherwise I suppose I'm lucky to be alive.'

'Hmm. Luckier than most, I'd say. From what I've heard, it was pretty horrific out there.' Theo carefully examined the man. 'From the look of your dented crash helmet, you took a hefty bang on the head.'

'Head like a brick, my wife says.' James attempted a chuckle and then placed a hand to his chest as a spasm of pain caught him. 'Stubborn and…' He paused as his breathing became more difficult. 'Mule headed, she always tells me. She doesn't like me having a motorbike.'

Theo smiled at that. 'We've been trying to get in touch with her to let her know what's happened,' he murmured. 'I gather she's not due at her work place for another hour, and she isn't at home either, so we'll keep trying.'

'I expect…' James paused again to gather breath. 'She'll be in her car.'

'That's probably it.' Theo ran his stethoscope over the man's chest, and then glanced at the nurse assisting him. 'Let's get an X-ray of the chest, Beth, followed by a CT scan of both the head and chest.' He glanced at his patient once more. 'Are you having trouble with your breathing?'

'Some.' James was really struggling now. 'My wife… We were…um… Bike was…' He appeared to be confused, and then he stopped speaking altogether, battling to pull breath into his lungs, a frightened look coming into his eyes.

Theo reached out to support him. 'I believe your lung must have collapsed,' he told him. 'I'm going to put in a drainage tube to relieve the pressure in there.'

James nodded an acknowledgment and Theo worked swiftly, swabbing the side of the man's chest and injecting a painkiller before attempting to insert the tube into an incision between the ribs. It would serve to drain off any build-up of blood in the pleural cavity that was threatening the lung.

James seemed to relax as the lung inflated once more, while Theo checked the outlet valve to make sure that all was well.

'That seems to be positioned correctly. Would you tape that in place for me, Beth? I want to listen to his chest again, and then we can go ahead with the X-ray and scans.'

Beth nodded, and set to work.

Megan let out a soft sigh of relief as she continued to assess her own patient. Theo seemed to have things under control. She could see that small beads of perspiration had broken out on his brow, but he was coping well enough, and that was the main thing.

The woman Megan was treating was in a bad way, but she had managed to find the source of internal bleeding and had stabilised the fractured pelvis so that it would be safe to transfer her to the operating theatre.

'Is the orthopaedic surgeon ready for her?' she asked Rhianna.

'He said he would be down here in ten minutes.'

'That's good.' Megan went to check the drip that she had set up to deliver intravenous fluids to her patient, but as she was doing that she became aware that things were not going to plan in the neighbouring bay.

'His blood pressure's rising,' Beth was saying.

Theo checked the monitors. 'Yes. I've noticed that's been happening over the last few minutes. I've given him intravenous medication to try to counteract it, but it's not having the desired effect.'

'Do you think something else could be going on here?' Beth asked. 'Something we haven't found yet?'

'I'm almost sure of it,' Theo agreed, keeping his voice low and even.

A note of urgency came into Beth's voice. 'I think he's crashing.' As Megan glanced in her direction, she saw that Theo's patient had slumped, and it looked as though he had lost consciousness.

For a second or two Theo was perfectly still. His jaw was taut, and there was tension in every line of his body. Megan held her breath, uncertain whether or not he would be able to cope with this new challenge. After all, he had insisted that he wasn't ready to come back to work, and for an awful instant she wondered if that was true. A wave of guilt washed over her. Had she done the wrong thing in persuading him that it was appropriate for him to be there? Perhaps she ought to ready herself to step in and take over… She stiffened, telling herself that it was the right thing to do. But she held back for a moment, concerned about the effect that would have on Theo when his confidence was already at risk.

All at once, though, he seemed to brace himself and swung into action. 'I'm going to put a tube in his throat to support his airway,' he said, tilting back the head of the bed and moving swiftly to check the man's windpipe. 'We need to get him on oxygen, fast.'

As soon as he had completed the procedure, he turned to Beth. 'Let's get him down to Radiology.'

Beth nodded, looking pale. 'What do you think is wrong with him?'

'I suspect he has multiple chest fractures, so we need to go carefully with him.' Theo grimaced. 'There must be internal injuries of some sort. All his vital signs are beginning to read that way, and we need to act quickly.'

Megan watched them wheel the patient away and went to supervise her own patient's transfer to Theatre. Her emotions were mixed. On the one hand she was relieved that any intervention on her part had been unnecessary, and Theo had risen to the occasion, but this was all turning out to be far more fraught than she had imagined. Would Theo be able to keep on top of his patient's care? When a patient who had suffered a blunt chest injury suddenly collapsed that way, it was a sign that something was badly wrong.

Theo couldn't help but be aware of that, and it showed in his manner. He was becoming more and more tense with each moment that passed, and she wished that there was some way she could ease his load without overstepping the mark.

While she waited for him to come back from Radiology, she busied herself checking on the other patients who had been brought in. One of the men suffering from leg trauma was losing consciousness, and she helped Sarah to wheel him into Resus.

'Keep a check on his fluid levels,' she told Sarah. 'I need to find out if there's a bleed that we've missed.'

She had just finished cauterising the troublesome blood vessel when Theo returned with his patient. Beth went to the phone and it became clear that she was trying once more to get in touch with James's wife. The nurse had a brief conversation with the woman on the other end of the line, and then she replaced the receiver.

'Is she coming in?' Megan asked.

Beth nodded. 'I just hope she's not too late.'

'Why…? What's happened?' She could see that Beth was shaken. 'What did the scans reveal?' Megan kept her voice low, not wanting to disturb Theo, who was tending his patient, his features a mask of concern and apprehension.

'Theo says there's evidence that he's bleeding from a major blood vessel of the heart. There are multiple fractures to the chest, and he called the surgeon over for a consultation. When Mr Carlson saw the scans he said the man needs open-heart surgery, but he probably wouldn't survive the operation. There are too many fractures and bone fragments, along with the damage to his lung, and the head injury is causing complications.'

'It's that bad?'

Beth nodded. 'The blood vessel to the heart has ballooned under pressure and ruptured so that blood is seeping out. Mr Carlson said the situation looked very grave. There was damage to the aortic arch, and that's very unusual, but if Theo was to operate on him he should prepare himself for the fact that things could go badly. Very few patients come safely through this sort of injury.'

Megan sucked in a deep breath. How could this be happening…his very first patient in mortal decline? It didn't bear thinking about, but if the respected consultant was ready to accept defeat, then it looked as though all was lost before they even began.

She glanced at Sarah. 'It looks as though our patient is making better headway now that the bleeding has stopped. I think he's stable enough to go to Theatre to have the bones in his leg fixed. Could I leave you to organise that? I should go and talk to Theo.'

'Yes, of course. You go.' Sarah's mouth flattened as she looked over at Theo's patient. They all knew how devastating the prognosis was.

Megan went to stand by Theo's side. 'Is there anything I can do to help?' She checked the monitors and the intravenous drips that, along with the oxygen delivery system, were giving Theo's patient the best chance of survival. 'Have you decided what you're going to do? Are you planning on operating?'

He seemed to straighten up. 'Yes,' he said. 'I'd be glad if you would come along and assist.'

Megan nodded. 'Of course.'

He glanced at Beth. 'We need to prep him for Theatre. I'm going to do an endovascular stent graft. That way, I don't need to open up the chest cavity. I can put the stent graft into position in the blood vessel by introducing a guide wire into the artery in his groin and then passing it through the circulatory system with the aid of the computer imagery.'

Beth's mouth dropped open and her eyes widened. Then, recovering, she said quickly, 'I'll go and get him ready.'

As she hurried away, Theo turned to look back at Megan. 'You're the expert in all that, so I'd appreciate your help. Perhaps you could monitor my progress on the computer?'

Megan nodded. 'I'd be glad to help. It sounds to me like a practical alternative to open-heart surgery. Let's do it.'

Beth assisted them throughout the procedure up in Theatre. The whole process took around an hour, and it was painstaking work, with Theo tense but composed throughout the entire exercise. There was quiet determination about him, as though he had made up his mind that failure was not an option and he was going to bring this patient through this terrible day by whatever means possible.

'That appears to be in position,' he said eventually. He glanced at the computer monitor. 'The stent should expand slightly now to shore up the wall of the artery. That's good. It seems to be working well.'

Megan gave a soft sigh of relief as the operation drew to a close. This last hour had been fraught with worry as they'd fought to save James, and now, at last, the slow bleed that had been causing his life to ebb away had been brought to a halt.

'You were wonderful,' she told Theo after they had wheeled James into the recovery room and left him with Beth to monitor his condition. 'You turned defeat into overwhelming success.'

'I wouldn't speak too soon if I were you,' Theo murmured, his face still taut from the stress of his exertions. 'He's not out of the woods yet. He still faces surgery tomorrow to fix and stabilise some of the fractures. Let's hope it all goes well.'

She smiled up at him. 'You've given him the very best chance possible,' she said softly. 'You should be proud of what you've achieved.' She put her arms around him and hugged him, a warm tide of happiness running through her.

His features remained taut, a muscle flicking in his jaw, darkness creeping into his eyes. 'I'm just doing what I can, but I still don't know that I can keep going.' His body was rigid, as though he was fighting off his demons, and she slowly broke away from him, watching him with a guarded expression.

'It was bound to be difficult for you,' she murmured. 'You always knew that, but at least you made an effort to start again. Surely you can grant yourself that?'

'I don't really want to think about it at all. I'm here, and that's all that can be said about it.' He straightened his shoulders as though he was bracing himself. 'All that really matters to me is that my sister should get better and come home to be a mother to Harry.'

Megan guessed that he was anxious to divert the conversation away from his attempt to come back into medicine, and she could well understand how he must be feeling. He had put himself under tremendous pressure, and it was taking everything he had to manage the situation. Megan's heart went out to him. She couldn't help but respect him for his courage in being there, and for the moment she would go along with whatever he needed to make his life easier.

'How is she?' she asked. 'I rang the stroke unit to ask after her, but they wouldn't tell me anything because I'm not a relative.'

'Really? I'll have a word with them about that. They're just being cautious, of course, as is proper. Actually, she's responding quite well to the treatment, and the pneumonia is clearing up. They've started on her physiotherapy, along with speech therapy. They want to get her up and about as soon as possible, even if it's only to transfer her to a wheelchair.'

'This must be difficult for Harry. How is he coping?'

'Well enough, I suppose.' He drew a deep breath. 'He's not saying very much at all, which is unusual in itself for Harry.'

'Is he still asking about a puppy? I seemed to have put my foot in it the other day when I assumed he had agreed to a rabbit, but maybe by now he's come around to your way of thinking?'

'Unfortunately, he hasn't. It's a bit of an ongoing battle.'

They walked towards the lift that would take them back down to A and E. Theo pressed the button and ushered her inside as the lift doors swung open.

'I would have asked you back to the house,' he said, 'but

things are in a state of upheaval at the moment, with the kitchen wall being knocked out and a layer of brick dust over everything.'

Her brows rose. 'You went ahead with the changes, then?' He nodded, and she said thoughtfully, 'That was quick work. You don't let the grass grow under your feet, do you?'

He nodded. 'I prefer to keep busy. It helps stop me from thinking too deeply.'

She looked up at him, her heart filled with a need to offer him solace of some kind. 'I wish there was something I could do to help.'

More than anything she would have liked to hold him, to wrap her arms around him and tell him that nothing in the world mattered except that he should keep his family close and realise that she was there for him, but she resisted the temptation.

He was locked into his own thoughts, his demeanour somehow forbidding, as though he would keep himself apart from everyone, and she knew this was not the time to draw him out.

Perhaps she had already pushed him too far.

CHAPTER NINE

'DO YOU think it will work out well enough for you, this system that John has set up…being on call with the ambulance service?' Megan finished writing up a prescription for beta-blockers and looked briefly at Theo before handing the chart over to Beth. The nurse moved away, heading back to the treatment bay.

'I expect so. I'm going to be working one week out of the month alongside the paramedics, starting today.' Theo's concentration was centred on a sheaf of lab-test results, but he sent Megan a quick glance. 'I'm based at the hospital, but if a really serious case arises, Rhianna will let me know and I'll go out from here.' He frowned. 'Things don't work that way for you, do they? You work a voluntary system, so you're called out from home during your off-duty periods.'

She nodded. 'It was a great advance for you to have it written into your contract. It means that management finally understands the need for doctors to be on emergency callout, and that's why they've given the go-ahead for a trial of the new system. It's brilliant, because it's what I've been working for all these months, and now, because of you, it looks as though I'll get to work under the same terms.'

'Really?' His mouth curved. 'I'm glad to have been of service.'

'Oh, you have, believe me.' Her features lit up with enthusiasm. 'Not just in getting that off the ground, but just by being here. You've been such a wonderful addition to the team over these last few weeks.'

Theo's face straightened as though he had reservations about that, but it was true enough as far as she was concerned. Spring had turned into summer, and Theo's first month on the job had been everything that she might have wished for. More than anything it had brought them closer to one another, and she realised that she loved having Theo by her side day after day.

Whatever doubts he might have about taking the job on, at least he was sticking to the schedule, and each day Megan held onto the hope that he was becoming a little more at ease with the situation than he had been the day before. He hadn't given any major clue as to what he was feeling in that regard. It was hard to know what was going through his mind and she had the impression he was simply getting on with things, forcing himself to do the job in the best way he could.

She reached for a radiology report from the tray on the desk and briefly scanned the contents.

'As I understood things,' Theo said, 'I won't actually be going out with the paramedics. I'll be using a fast-response car that's equipped with everything I might need.'

'Yes, I heard about that. In fact, John asked me to go with you, so that I can smooth your path, if you like. It'll be great for me, because it means I'll get to see the new scheme in operation. He wants me to report on how it works, and note down any changes that I think might be needed to make things go more smoothly. He's hoping that if things turn out well, it might become a permanent feature of the way we work in the trust area.'

'It sounds as though your efforts have borne fruit.' He

smiled at her, and for a moment or two it was as though no one else in the world existed but the two of them. She basked in that smile, letting it warm her through and through.

'They have. I'm thrilled to bits with the way things are going.' She was content, too, that Theo was still there, still part of her everyday life.

She sent him a quick glance. 'How will you manage things with Harry if you're to be out on call? He'll be coming home from school, won't he, while you're still on duty?'

'My parents will collect him for me, and keep him with them overnight. It won't happen this way too often because of the way things are scheduled, but I agreed to the timetable, so it doesn't put me out too much. Harry loves being with his grandparents, and they love having him.'

'That must be a relief for you, though I think you're doing a marvellous job with him, taking care of him the way you do.' Her brows drew together and her mouth took on a solemn slant. 'I don't know if I could ever cope with holding a family together. I would be so worried that I might do the wrong thing. Children can be so vulnerable at times, and I'm not sure I would be able to handle things well enough.' She hadn't even been able to establish rapport with Harry.

He looked at her oddly. 'Do you never think of getting married and having children of your own?'

It disturbed her to think about that question. Wasn't it something she had turned over in her mind many times before this? She put down the radiology report she was reading and became very still as she answered. 'I don't know about that. I'm not sure things will ever work out that way for me.'

'But you've had boyfriends in the past, haven't you? Everybody around here is very fond of you and it would be hard to imagine that someone as caring and friendly as you had never been deeply involved with anyone. The thought must have crossed your mind at some time.' He was watching her through narrowed eyes, as though he was trying to puzzle her out.

'Maybe, but so far things haven't worked out for me relationship-wise.' In truth, Theo was the only man who had ever managed to pierce her defences, and the effect he had on her was thoroughly confusing. Ever since he had come into her life, her emotions had been continuously at odds with one another. It was very unsettling.

She said on a cautious note, 'It isn't always easy to find someone who is on the same wavelength as me, and perhaps I find it too hard to believe that people have real staying power. Somehow or other, over the years, I've been let down by the people I've become fond of. Perhaps that's my fault. Maybe I expect too much.'

She gave a light shrug. 'Either way, I don't really have any particularly good experiences to fall back on, and I tend to worry about whether things would work out long term.'

She hesitated, her teeth worrying at the fullness of her lower lip. 'I get on well with everyone here, as you say, and they have become wonderful friends, people I trust. As to family and children, I've tried not to think about that too much. I'd like to think that everyone gets their happy ever after, but it wasn't that way for my parents, and the thought that any children of mine could be left to flounder the way I did has always bothered me. I wouldn't want to put them through that.'

He studied her thoughtfully, his head tilted to one side. 'Aren't you tending to look on the black side?'

'You're probably right.' Her mouth twisted into a lopsided curve. 'I want to be like other people, but the things I care about most of all have been snatched away from me and I suppose I'm afraid that history will repeat itself.'

His hand went lightly around her waist. 'Strange creature. You're beautiful, in looks and in nature, and you have everything going for you, and yet you see life as a closed book. You know I think the world of you. Perhaps you should take a leap in the dark and soar freely for once.'

Her heart warmed at his words, but she knew that she shouldn't read too much into them. 'Of course I will,' she murmured, giving him a sweet smile. 'Will you provide the parachute?'

He laughed, and his hand slipped away from her as he gave his attention back to his lab results.

For Megan's part, she tried to concentrate on her radiology report once more, but her flesh was on fire where his hand had rested, and all she could think was that he made her heart pound and he stirred her blood like no man before him. But what was the use in looking to him as a soulmate? He might well be just what the doctor ordered, but he had more than enough on his plate, and he probably didn't have any notion of how he managed to heat her blood with a mere glance in her direction.

She made herself concentrate on the work in hand, and later she was attending to a patient when the first callout came just after lunch.

'There's been an accident at a local tourist spot, the Lakeside Falls,' Rhianna told Megan. 'It happened as a young couple were climbing rocks close by the edge of the fall. They were trying to get a closer look, according to people who were nearby, when the young woman slipped and fell some of the way down. I don't know how difficult it's going to be to get in to treat her, but they've called for a rescue team.'

Theo was already on the move. 'I know the place,' he said. 'We'll probably be able to get to her via the lane that runs close by the lake.'

They both handed over their patients to colleagues and hurried away. Theo drove swiftly to the accident spot, some five miles away from the hospital. Once they had gone as far as they could by road, he parked the car, and they discovered that the ambulance had arrived at much the same time.

'We've called out the mountain rescue team,' the chief paramedic, Ryan, told them, 'but they're already out on a search for a missing youngster, so they'll have to locate members of the team and send anyone they can spare.'

'That doesn't sound too promising, does it?' Megan was already concerned that the woman might be lying badly injured and in need of immediate help.

Theo shook his head. 'If she's halfway down the waterfall, maybe we could find the footpath that follows the river. It's not well used, but it should take us part way down the slope, and it will get us in closer to her than the official route for sightseers.'

'You said you know the place…have you been here recently?' Megan asked.

'Not recently, but we came here a lot when we were growing up. And when I've been down visiting my parents I've come down here from time to time.'

Together with the paramedics, they scrambled over rough terrain, following the directions the woman's husband had given them, to the site where the woman had fallen. It was heavy going, hampered as they were by the medical equipment they were carrying, and after a while Megan found her breath was coming in short bursts.

'It could be worse,' Theo murmured. 'At least we have good, dry weather. It would be much more difficult to have to stretcher her back over wet ground.'

As it was, when they finally came across the woman, they

saw that she was slumped on a craggy outcrop of rock where the conditions were hazardous in the extreme. The tumbling cascade of the waterfall was frothing to one side of her, and the rugged surface of the ground was wet and slippery as they tried to approach.

Her husband was waiting further down the slope at the official access point, and now he signalled to them his relief that they had arrived and indicated the place where she had fallen.

Theo stood on a flat stretch of volcanic rock and looked down to where she lay. 'She appears to be losing a lot of blood, and she's not answering when I call to her,' he said, his voice grim. 'We don't have time to wait for the mountain rescue team to arrive. I'll see if I can get over there to her.'

'It isn't safe, without the proper equipment,' Megan put in quickly as he started forward. To reach the woman, he would have to negotiate the rocks and wooded slope, and below them the foaming waters formed a whirlpool at the base of the rocks several feet below. It didn't bear thinking about if he were to fall.

'I brought some rope with me just in case it was needed,' he said, his voice preoccupied. 'I decided a while back to add a few things to the equipment that was already in the car.' He frowned. 'Maybe we could rig something up.' He glanced towards the paramedics. 'Do you think we could find a way to fix the rope in place? Then if I tie the other end around my waist and shoulders, I could lower myself down to her.'

'We should be able to fix it around that jutting crag,' Nick, the second paramedic said, indicating a nearby ridge. 'Are you sure you're going to be able to handle this?'

Theo nodded. 'I've had some experience with climbing. You might need to lower extra equipment down to me, though. There's only so much this medical bag will hold.'

'I'm sure we'll manage to sort something out.'

They worked as a team to secure the rope, but Megan's heart was in her mouth the whole time. What would she do if anything was to happen to him? What would become of Harry if Theo was hurt?

Some time later Theo completed the descent and steadied himself on the rock ledge where the injured woman was lying. He made a brief examination. 'She's unconscious and bleeding from a chest wound,' he called up to them. 'I'm going to put in an airway and try to stem the bleeding. Then I'll need to set up an intravenous line to replace the fluids she's lost.'

He worked swiftly, and then said, 'I'll need splints for her leg…it looks as though she has a fracture.'

Megan worked with the paramedics to send down the equipment he needed, using the rope that was supporting him as a transit for the splints, hooking them onto the line with their Velcro fastenings so that they slid down towards him. She wished she could go down there and join him, but with only one rope it was impossible.

She began to fret. It was too cramped on that ledge for him to be able to work safely. What if he missed his footing? At the very least he would be dashed against the rocks. How could they be sure that the rope would hold?

If only the mountain rescue team would arrive. Surely they would have everything that was needed?

It was some fifteen minutes, though, before the rescuers finally put in an appearance, and she gave a ragged sigh of relief.

They set up their equipment, and began to organise a pulley system for the stretcher. 'We'll need spinal support,' Theo told them. 'Until we get her to hospital for scans we can't tell what damage might have been done. She has a nasty head injury as well.'

The whole operation took around an hour, and when they finally winched the woman up to safety, Megan could see clearly that she was in a bad way. Theo had done everything he could for her, but she was weak from blood loss, and unresponsive.

The paramedics tended to her, checking her airway and making sure that the splints were correctly in place. 'Her heart rhythm is chaotic,' Ryan said, 'but her oxygen level is coming up. We need to get her to hospital as soon as possible.'

Between them, they carried her stretcher back to the waiting ambulance. Within moments the vehicle's blue light was flashing and the woman was on her way to A and E.

'Thanks for everything that you did to get her out of there,' Megan said to the rescue team. 'It was a difficult rescue, and you were all marvellous. Even so, I can't help worrying that we called you away from another mission.'

'It's all in a day's work,' the team leader said. 'But you're right, we need to get back to our search for the missing child.'

'What happened? How did the child come to be missing?' Megan was racked with concern.

'He left his house after an argument with his parents, and they've no idea where he might be. He's only thirteen years old. Apparently they fell out over his schoolwork and the time he spends playing computer games. He isn't with his friends, so they thought he might have gone wandering over the valley and exploring the hill slopes, so we're concentrating our search on those areas.'

She nodded. 'That sounds logical. How long has he been missing?'

'Since some time last night. They sent him up to bed after the row, but he wasn't in his room when his mother went to check on him this morning. He must have sneaked out when they were asleep.'

She grimaced, saddened by the episode. 'His parents must be in a terrible state.'

'They are.'

She and Theo waited while the rescuers packed up their equipment. Then they waved them off before going over to their own car.

Theo was very quiet, and it occurred to Megan that his manner had been subdued ever since the woman had been brought up to level ground once more.

'I was so worried about you,' she said, sending him an oblique glance. 'It was so dangerous back there, and I kept thinking that you might slip at any moment. You could have been dashed against the rocks at any time, even with the rope around you.'

'I was fine, and the rope held up, so you needn't have worried.' He tried a smile, but she could see that he was on edge and under a good deal of strain, and she wondered if the effort of working against all the odds to save the woman had brought back his former doubts about what he was doing. His face was shadowed and the line of his jaw was taut.

She put her arms around him and gazed up into his troubled blue eyes. 'You were incredibly brave to do what you did. You probably saved that woman's life.'

He frowned. Even as his arms reached for her in response, his body was rigid, tension evident in every sinew. 'There's no knowing how she'll do. She has a head injury along with all her other problems. She'll be lucky to survive that, let alone the broken leg and smashed ribs.'

'But you did what you could for her, and that's what counts, isn't it? If we'd waited for the rescue team she might have died right there. Without you doing what you did, she wouldn't have stood a chance.'

She lifted her face to him, wanting only to hold him and comfort him and show him that the world held all kinds of possibilities if only he would seek them out. The fact that the woman had a head injury must have reminded him vividly of his sister's unhappy state. She wanted so much to take his mind off all his worries, and more than anything, she wanted to kiss him right there and then.

Perhaps he read her thoughts because he began to lower his head towards her, brushing his lips against hers hesitantly, holding back, as though a war was raging within his body. Then, with a ragged, shuddery breath, he deepened the kiss, as though he could not help himself, as though the fire that sparked inside him was being stoked into flame.

Megan's body melted into his, the softness of her curves crushed against him as he pulled her into the hard bulwark of his body. 'You make me feel so good,' he muttered, his voice roughened. 'I can't get enough of you. Being with you like this makes it seem as though nothing else matters. I just want to hold you and kiss you and never let you go.'

'That sounds just about perfect to me,' she murmured softly. 'I love being in your arms. You make me feel as though this is where I belong.'

He laughed, a gentle, husky sound that rumbled in the back of his throat. 'Perhaps you do,' he murmured. 'I've never felt this way before…wanted something so much…felt so complete…You're beautiful and warm and womanly, thoughtful, caring and gentle…everything a man could wish for.' He smiled down at her. 'I think I must be falling in love with you, Megan.' His hand lifted and he lightly stroked her cheek. 'What am I to do about the way I feel?'

'Give in to it,' she answered softly, loving the way his body sheltered hers, the way his arms coaxed her to cling to him for support. Was he really falling in love with her? That sounded wonderful to her, and she was in heaven in his embrace, her whole world suddenly filled with sunshine.

Obligingly, his hands shaped her, exploring the rounded contours of her slender form as he drew her into the shade of a nearby tree. The branches hung down, shielding them from view, and Megan lost herself in the warmth of his embrace. This was sheer bliss, being here with him this way, wrapped in his arms.

She tilted her face to him and he dropped tender kisses over her forehead, the bridge of her nose, her cheeks, before claiming her mouth once more. She kissed him in return, her lips clinging to his, the heat of passion running through her entire body.

His fingers splayed out over her rib cage and travelled slowly upwards, until his thumb cupped the soft weight of her breast and she pulled in a quick breath as flame ran through her from head to toe. His hand slid over her, tracing a delicate line over the fullness of her curves, until a soft moan of pleasure escaped her and he looked down at her once more.

Perhaps the small sound she made had the effect of bringing him back to his senses, or maybe it was the rustle of leaves on the trees, the faint crackle of twigs underfoot that made him pause. She wondered if other people were about.

He drew in a sharp breath, his whole body becoming tense once more. 'I'm sorry,' he muttered. 'I don't know what I was thinking. I was carried away, but this is neither the time nor the place. I should never have started any of this.'

Shaken, she looked up at him. 'It was my fault,' she whispered. 'Seeing what you did back there…I just wanted to hold you. You looked so…bereft somehow, and I wanted to make things right. I've pushed you into taking on this job and

I hoped that you would feel good about it, but that doesn't seem to be happening.'

'You can't do anything to alter the way I feel,' he said flatly. 'And you don't need to try. In the end, it was my decision to come back to work, my choice.'

He straightened. 'Besides, I'm not sure that it has been altogether a bad thing. It has been a difficult path to tread, that's true enough, and at times I've wondered if I was doomed to fail, but underneath it all I've begun to realise that this is what I need to do. Helping that woman today has made me see things more clearly. I'm always going to worry in case things go wrong—there's always going to be that tightness and fear running through me—but I can't let it shut me down. I have to accept it for what it is, the natural consequence of what life throws at us. I have to deal with it and work through it and do whatever I can to help people to survive, even if I might not always succeed.'

He straightened, as though he was making an effort to pull himself together once more. 'Besides, we made a deal, didn't we? Weren't you going to pose for me? I still have a hankering to paint you…and it seems to me that this evening would be a fine time to start. What do you say? Will you be free to do that?'

Her eyes widened. How could she do anything but agree? She wanted only to be with him, to share his life, and make everything right. He had said that he thought he was falling in love with her and that made her brim over with happiness, even as she wondered if he had merely been caught up with all the passion of the moment. Today had been a testing time for him, with his emotions driven to the edge by the drama of the rescue and the worry about the woman's condition, and given all that, he might not be sure what it really was that he felt for her. Even though instinct told her she could only be hurt by the way things might turn out, she was powerless to resist.

* * *

The rest of the afternoon passed in a whirl as they went back to work. There was a second callout to attend a road traffic accident, and almost before she realised it, it was time for her shift to end.

She went home and made preparations for the evening ahead.

As soon as Megan arrived at Theo's house around an hour later, her doubts returned. Where was the wisdom of agreeing to this?

Whatever had happened near the waterfall that afternoon seemed to be part of another existence now. It had been madness to hold him the way she had, when clearly his mind had been overtaken by the seriousness of the situation and the stress of everything they had been through had still been hanging over him.

Perhaps she should remind him of that from the outset. Then there would be no misunderstandings between them, and the folly of the afternoon would be seen for what it was, a mistake, foolishness on her part because she had been overcome by a need to offer him comfort. The fact that she loved him was neither here nor there, was it?

There, she had said it again. Not to him, but to herself. She did love him, she was sure of that now, but it was one thing to admit that to herself and quite another to do anything about it.

'I'm glad you were able to come over,' he said, showing her into the kitchen where a pot of hot coffee was brewing, filling the air with its wonderful aroma. 'I had the feeling you might back out on me.'

She sent him a surreptitious glance from under her lashes. 'Why would you have that idea?'

He made a wry smile. 'I know that you didn't intend things to go as far as they did this afternoon. You were in an emotional state after everything that had gone on—the woman badly injured and a child missing.'

He frowned. 'A kiss is just a kiss, but things got out of hand. I came on too strong, too suddenly, and I should have known better. I know you have problems with getting in too deep. You said as much a while back, but I didn't really take it on board, and this afternoon I wasn't thinking too clearly, or it wouldn't have happened.'

'Wouldn't it?' She had her own reservations about getting close to him, but when she was in his arms her mind seemed to push aside all the warnings her body was sending out to her. How was it that he had seen what she had missed? Was that the reality of it, or was he giving them both a chance to back out, because he had discovered that he was simply not as taken with her as she was with him?

'I wasn't myself this afternoon,' he said. 'I was worried about the woman who fell. The head injury reminded me of what had happened to Francie, especially as the woman was of a similar age. It's such a tragedy in someone so young, with her life ahead of her.'

'I wondered if it might be something like that…but I was afraid there was more to it. You might have been regretting starting the job in the first place. I was run through with guilt, because I felt as though I had pushed you into it. You've been so quiet and absorbed in other things these last few weeks that I guessed you weren't comfortable with the way the job was going.'

His shoulders made an awkward shrug. 'None of it is your fault. I haven't been able to give my full attention to anything of late. Things seem to be slipping away from me, what with starting work and watching out for Harry. He's anxious about his mother, and it's a job and a half to keep him from being discouraged.'

'Is she not making any headway?' She leaned back against the worktop, watching as he prepared mugs of coffee, adding cream and sugar in exactly the way she liked. It seemed that nothing escaped him. Once told, it was a lesson he remembered for ever, as with other things he had discovered about her. She wasn't sure how she felt about that.

'She's beginning to improve little by little, but it's a slow process. We've learned to take one day at a time—at least, I have. It's not quite so easy for Harry.'

'So she won't be coming home for a while yet?'

He shook his head. 'They won't send her home until they can be sure she'll be able to get about safely. When the time comes I'll bring her back here, so that she can be near to our parents. It means that I'll have to make arrangements to have handrails fitted in the house and aids about the place to help her cope with everyday living. That, in itself, will take some time to organise.'

'It must be wonderful for her to have a family who care so much about her. Is she able to talk to you about how she feels?'

'She can manage a few words. The speech therapist works with her every day, and the physiotherapist does likewise. Of all of the help she receives, though, I think Harry's input does her the most good.'

Megan sent him a quizzical look. 'Because he cheers her up?'

'Yes, and because he gives her the incentive to get well. She wants to be able to hold him and do all the things that she used to do with him, but she becomes frustrated by her physical state. Harry chats away to her and it's hard to keep up with him sometimes. He forgets that she can't move her arm properly and that she can't walk by herself.'

'That's so sad.'

'We just have to stay positive. What she needs is encouragement and people around her.' He gave her a thoughtful look. 'Perhaps you'd like to come with me to see her one day? She'd be glad of company, especially people of her own age.'

'I'd like that.'

'Good.' He handed her a mug of coffee. 'Shall we go up to the studio? The light's still good and I could make a start on a few sketches.'

'All right.' She glanced around the kitchen. 'You've made this look absolutely perfect, by the way. I love the new archway into the dining room.' Glancing through the open space into the dining area, she saw that the furniture had been arranged to perfection in there, and everything looked as though it had been designed especially for that room. 'It's so light in there, too.'

He nodded. 'It was always reasonably light in there with the French doors, but the sun pours in through the kitchen window at a different angle and brightens up the whole area. I discovered it was an added bonus and, as you said, it's good to be able to sit in there and have breakfast while looking out over the garden.'

'I can imagine it would be.' She gave an inward sigh. Wouldn't it be even more wonderful if she was able to share that experience with him?

She took a last look around and then followed him up the stairs to the studio. In there, he had placed a rocking chair by the window, adding cushions to make it even more comfortable.

'Have a seat,' he said. 'I'll get my sketch pad.'

She did as he'd suggested, testing out the chair and easing herself back into it. 'Oh,' she murmured. 'This is wonderful. I could just sit here for ever. It's so relaxing after a hard day's

work. It's absolute bliss.' She looked across the room at him
and he returned the smile, but he was already busy sketching,
his charcoal moving across the page in short, swift strokes.

She hadn't been certain what she ought to wear for this
sitting. Perhaps he was only intending to do a head-and-shoul-
ders portrait, but the fact that he had chosen this chair for her
to sit in suggested otherwise. In any event, she had decided
on a gently swirling skirt and a softly draped cotton top, in
keeping with the warmth of the summer evening.

He was absorbed in his work, talking to her as he sketched,
undemanding, simply allowing her to be herself, and after a
while she relaxed, letting her thoughts wander. He made
several drawings, one after the other, his expression intent,
totally focussed on what he was doing.

She had been sitting there for about an hour when the
phone rang, disturbing the peace.

Theo put down his charcoal. 'I expect that will be Harry,
wanting to say goodnight. Anyway, maybe it's a good time
for us take a break. Stretch your legs if you want to.'

She nodded, stretching her whole body sinuously, like a
kitten enjoying a laze in the sunshine. 'Is there any chance I
could see the sketches?'

'Perhaps not just yet.' His manner was guarded as he walked
over to the phone. 'I need to work on them some more.'

It was Harry on the other end of the line, as he had guessed.
She only heard Theo's side of the conversation, but she
gathered that Harry was having a good time at his grandparents' house, and they had set up a train set that used to belong
to Theo when he was a child so that Harry could play with it.
Theo's father and mother put in comments from time to time,
and Theo was chuckling as he listened.

Eventually, he put down the receiver and turned to Megan.

'It sounds as though my father's had as much fun from the train set as Harry,' he told her. 'They've set up signals, and added tunnels for the trains to go through, and even made the track rise and fall in places. It almost makes me wish I was a child again.'

Megan smiled. 'It was good to hear you all talking together. It was very clear that there is such a lot of love between all of you. That's something very special.'

He nodded, and went to gather up his papers and tidy up the assortment of charcoal sticks he had set aside.

Megan strolled over to the window and looked out over the garden. She could imagine children out there on the smooth expanse of lawn, playing hide and seek among the trees or in the shrubbery. This was a big house, made for a family. Had Theo once played down there?

Her thoughts wandered to the child who had gone missing that morning. Did he have brothers and sisters, or was he an only child? What could have been going through his mind to make him want to run away?

'You're very quiet.' Theo came to stand beside her, gazing out at the wide sweep of the garden. 'Is something wrong?' He sent her a thoughtful glance, taking in the straightened line of her mouth.

'I was thinking about the child who went missing. I rang the rescue services to see if they had managed to find him, but they were still out looking. I thought about joining the search, but there wasn't really time after we finished work.'

'We must have been thinking along similar lines. I rang them just before you arrived here, and it turns out that he's all right…none the worse for wear. They came across him about a couple of hours ago, huddled into a cave some three miles from his home. He was tired and hungry, but otherwise he's fine.'

Megan heaved a sigh of relief. 'I'm so glad about that. It was on my mind all the time…I couldn't help wondering what he was going through, whether his parents would be able to handle the situation.'

'They were overjoyed to be reunited with him.' Theo's mouth curved. 'These family skirmishes seem to arise out of nothing and get blown out of all proportion. Teenagers can be volatile at the best of times.'

'I hope they manage to sort things out.'

'I'm sure they will. The boy's father was beside himself with worry, afraid that he had gone too far and driven the boy away. I suppose it has served as a wake-up call all round.'

'It's a good result.'

'Yes.' He slid an arm around her shoulders. 'It obviously upset you. Was that because it made you think back over your own family background?'

'I suppose so. Hearing you talking with your parents and Harry brought it all home to me in a way. I don't know what it's like to be part of all that.'

'I can imagine that must be difficult for you. Do you see much of your father? You hardly ever talk about him.'

'We keep in touch. He lives some twenty miles from here, and I see him on a fairly regular basis, though we were never all that close. It was as though we were both holding something back, I suppose. We had both been hurt.'

'Hmm.' His gaze wandered over her features. 'I guessed as much. Do you want to tell me about it?'

Megan was glad of his arm around her. It was an embrace that said, Lean on me. I care about you. I'm here for you. And her body warmed in response to his touch.

'There's nothing much to tell. He brought me up and made sure that I had everything I needed…in a material sense…but there was a lot of resentment after my mother left. You could almost feel it, simmering in the atmosphere. My father was tense and unhappy and didn't talk very much. For a long time I blamed myself because she had gone. I thought I must have been very bad to be so unloved.'

She pressed her lips together briefly. 'Then, when I was older, I blamed my father for not going after her or making an effort to persuade her to come back. I was very mixed up. I didn't really know how to cope with the situation, and it simply festered, driving a wedge between us.'

Theo drew her into the shelter of his body, his lips lightly brushing her cheek. 'You could never have been unloved. It doesn't make any sense at all to think that way. No one who knows you could fail to love you.'

His mouth sought hers and he kissed her tenderly, drawing from her all the pent-up emotion that threatened to over-whelm her. Her lips softened, clung, and for a while it was like a taste of heaven, being here with him, having him hold her and kiss her this way.

After a few minutes, though, he reluctantly broke off the kiss, easing himself back from her a little.

His glance travelled over her face. 'Is it possible that your father's unhappiness might have coloured your thinking? Perhaps he was bitter about her leaving and made the situation seem worse than it was. She might not have been the guilty party. He might have put his own slant on things, and you, being young, believed him. Maybe you should try to find your mother and hear what she has to say for herself.'

'No, I can't do that.' Her response was immediate, the words coming out more sharply than she intended. 'I don't want to do that. I've had enough of waiting and hoping and all of it coming to nothing.'

'But I could help you,' Theo said. 'We could do this together. You wouldn't have to go through it alone.'

Disturbed, she laid a hand on his rib cage and gradually drew back from him. He didn't understand what it had been like for her after her mother's departure, or how the desertion had struck through her like a knife to the heart.

'No. No one can help me. It isn't the way you think. I knew from the letters I had from her over the years that I was wishing for the moon. At first I was full of hope, but then gradually I began to see things as they really were.'

She heaved in a shuddery breath. 'The letters were always about herself…what she was doing, where she was heading, what was going on in her life, as though I would be swept along by that and be happy for her. There was hardly anything to show that she cared about what I was feeling, or what I might be doing… Or about my father.'

'So it's still all up in the air. Nothing has been resolved for you on that score, but you clearly need to have some kind of closure after all that's gone on. How are you ever going to live your life to the full if you're always looking back over your shoulder?' Theo was concerned for her, and it showed in his taut features and in the way his gaze searched her face. 'Perhaps I could help you to sort things out with your family once and for all. I want to show you that I'm here for you, Megan, in any way I can.'

'No. It isn't possible.' Her voice was shaky, and she was beginning to feel panicky as all her former angst came back to haunt her. 'If I've learned anything, it's that people let you down. Nothing is ever safe and secure, and it doesn't do to rely on anyone.' She stepped away from him. 'Life can't be put right in the way that you think. It just doesn't work that way.'

'But I wouldn't let you down. I'll be there for you, no

matter what. It would just take a little courage on your part to set things in motion.'

She took another step backwards. 'No, I won't do it. I won't go through all that upset and upheaval all over again. I've accepted what happened, and I've come to realise that there's nothing I can do about it. I won't put my trust in anyone ever again. You can't ask me to do that.'

She looked at him, wanting to accept what he was saying but knowing that it was impossible. She had been hurt badly in the past, and she would never put herself through that again. Even Theo, well intentioned though he may be, would let her down at some point. Everyone did.

'I don't need you to look out for me,' she told him. 'I don't need anybody. I can take care of myself. I'm better off on my own. I should never have let myself get involved with you in the first place outside work. I knew it was a mistake.'

Theo was staring at her, his expression impossible to read, his features rigid with tension. 'You don't mean that,' he said. 'You don't know what you're saying.'

'That's just it. I do. I know exactly what it means to love someone and have them betray your trust.' Her voice was thready with emotion. 'I tried for a long time to make some sense of my mother leaving. I couldn't understand how she could be the way she was. I still find it hard, to this day, and I made up my mind that I wouldn't ever let myself be that vulnerable ever again.'

She started towards the door, needing to escape the turmoil that clouded her thinking. 'I need to go,' she said. 'I have to get ready for tomorrow. We have another long day ahead of us.'

He moved as though he would stop her, but she was already through the door and heading downstairs. 'Megan, wait…'

'No.' She turned at the foot of the stairs. 'You need to back off, Theo. I can't do this.' Then she hurried out of the door.

For a while, in his arms, she had allowed herself to be lured into a false sense of security, but that had been a mistake. Life had never turned out for her the way she had hoped. There was always this feeling that the rug might be pulled out from under her feet.

What had she been doing here with Theo, allowing herself to think that somehow she would get her happy ever after? Her thoughts were chaotic, and she was caught up in a maelstrom of doubts. She had to get away, to be alone for a while so that she could think things through and try to make sense of what was going on in her life.

CHAPTER TEN

'SHE'S doing really well, isn't she?' Sarah was reading a report from the newspaper about the woman Theo had rescued from the waterfall several weeks ago. 'It says here that she's full of praise for the team that saved her life.'

Megan glanced at the article. There hadn't been any journalists around when the event had been unfolding, but someone must have told the press, and since then Theo and the rescue team had been interviewed on a couple of occasions.

'I like the bit where John praises the paramedics and the mountain rescue service. He goes on to make the point that there are occasions when it's essential to have a highly skilled doctor present from the outset if the patient is to survive.' Megan's mouth made a rueful curve. 'I only hope the hospital trust board is sitting up and taking notice.'

'I'm sure they are. Theo has done wonders to raise the reputation of the department.'

'Yes, he has. He seems to have a sure touch with emergency surgery. Look at how he saved the motorcyclist when everyone thought he was done for. James made a wonderful recovery after Theo put in the stent graft. Although he had to have further surgery to repair the fractured bones the next day, it was all plain sailing after that.'

Just as the woman's health had improved over the weeks that had gone by, and she was regaining her strength little by little, so Theo appeared to be gaining in confidence. With each day that passed, his doubts appeared to be fading. His demeanour brightened, and every action he took made Megan realise what a motivating force he must have presented at his previous hospital. He was an inspiration to everyone who worked with him, and it had soon become obvious why John had always held him in such high regard.

Watching him at work, Megan was convinced that before much more time had passed he would begin to think long and hard about his future...a future that would not include her. After all, she had rebuffed him, hadn't she, making it perfectly clear that he needed to leave her be? And he had taken her at her word, backing right off and never once overstepping the mark by trying to kiss her or hold her, but always treating her as though he cared for her.

She knew, though, that his career was back on track, and she was certain that one day he would make his decision and prepare to move on.

Perhaps that was why she was guarded in her manner whenever she was in Theo's company. She still saw him away from A and E, going to his home for several sittings for the painting he was working on, and she even went with him and Harry to visit his sister in the stroke unit. All the time, though, she was aware that she needed to put up a defensive screen, one that would keep her from losing her heart to him completely and irrevocably.

'Theo's parents are here to see him, by the way.' Sarah's voice cut into Megan's thoughts. 'They said that they're here to visit their daughter as usual, but they wanted to stop by A and E to talk to Theo first. He's in Resus, but Rhianna has told him that they're here. Last I saw of them, they were waiting by the desk.'

'Really? Thanks for letting me know. I'll go and have a word with them.'

She walked over to the central desk where Theo's mother and father were waiting patiently.

'Hello. I heard that you were here,' she said, smiling. 'Theo is with a patient, but he'll be with you as soon as he's free.' She sent them a quizzical look. 'I know you come to see Francie most days, but this is the first time you've come into our unit, isn't it?'

Theo's father nodded. 'We don't want to disturb him unnecessarily.'

'Well, I'm sure he'll be pleased to see you. I'm Megan, by the way. Would you like me to show you around the place?'

'Thank you. That would be good, but only if you have the time.' Theo's father was tall, with the same blue eyes as his son, although his hair was greying now, streaks of silver lending him a dignified look. 'We didn't mean to put anybody out. I know how busy you are in here, but we wanted to let him know that we'll be going away for the weekend.' He smiled, glancing briefly at his wife. 'It was a bit of a last-minute decision, a trip to the coast to celebrate our anniversary.'

His wife was a slender woman, grey eyed, with a beautiful, oval-shaped face and features that reminded Megan of Francie. 'We need to tell him about it so that he can make arrangements for Harry. The lad comes to us sometimes at the weekend, but this is a special occasion for us, and we'll be meeting up with friends.'

'It sounds as though you're going to have fun,' Megan said. 'Let me show you Theo's paintings while you're waiting for him. They have pride of place in our waiting room and treatment bay, and people often comment on how lovely they are.'

'We'd like that.' Theo's mother looked at her appreciatively. 'Theo has talked a lot about you. You're the one who persuaded him to come back to work, aren't you? After he left his previous job, I was afraid that he would never go back to medicine. He kept things to himself, and none of us were able to draw him out. He just said that he would work things out in his own time, but before you came along he was becoming more and more withdrawn. All he wanted to do was work on his paintings, as though he was trying to blot everything else out.'

'It's amazing to see the difference in him now,' his father tacked on. 'He talks about being on call and what a difference it can make to be there with the patient within minutes of injury. He was even talking about the possibility of extending the system to other areas, and I know he's had an approach from his former chief at the hospital in Somerset, so that would be a start. They want him back there.' His mouth slanted. 'They want him in the States, too. A former colleague has been in touch with him from over there.'

'It sounds as though he has several options to consider.' Megan tried to keep up a cheerful appearance as she showed them around, but inside she was becoming more and more despondent.

Wasn't it what she had expected all along? His contract was due to end soon, and he would definitely have to start thinking about where he wanted to go next.

'I heard that Francie was getting on well with the physiotherapy,' she said, showing them into the waiting room where Theo's painting had pride of place. 'You must be very pleased about that. Does it mean that she'll be coming home soon?'

'It does.' His mother smiled. 'Of course, she'll need lots of help to begin with, and Theo is making arrangements for someone to be with her at the house and continue with the physiotherapy. It will be so good for Harry to have his mother back home with him. Of course, we don't know when that will be yet.'

That was good news, the very best, and they were right. Harry would be absolutely delighted.

She pushed her own feelings to the back of her mind and gave them a quick tour of the department. By the time she was finished, Theo was ready to greet them.

'It's good to see you both,' he said, nodding towards his father and giving his mother a hug. His brows drew together momentarily. 'Is this about your anniversary? I guessed you might be planning something.'

'We're going away…but we weren't sure if it would inter-fere with your plans. Didn't you say that you had to go down to Somerset?' His father was frowning.

'That's right. I've made arrangements with the agents to go and sort out the house this weekend,' Theo said. 'The tenancy is coming to an end, and I need to see that every-thing's in order for the next stage. Added to that, my former boss has invited me to attend a charity do at the hospital on Friday evening. He wanted to talk me through a proposition concerning a new contract. It means I'll have to stay there over the weekend.' His brows drew together as he thought things through. 'I dare say I'll be able to make arrangements for Harry. He could probably go and stay with a friend.'

'Or he could come to my place,' Megan offered. 'That way I could take him to see Francie. He doesn't like to miss out on a visit, does he? I wouldn't like to see him upset if it can be avoided.'

Theo turned to look at her. 'Are you sure you wouldn't mind doing that? I don't want to put you out at all.'

'It's no bother. I'm not on duty then, and Harry is fairly

used to being with me now, so it shouldn't worry him too much. Ask him what he'd prefer to do.'

Theo gave her a smile. 'I will. Thanks. You're an angel.'

Megan acknowledged that with a rueful twist to her mouth. He had no idea what she was really feeling, did he? He was going away, most likely to prepare for going back to live and work in Somerset, or even to sell up and leave the country altogether, and her heart was in pieces at the mere thought.

He would go without a backward glance, and the only time she might see him in the future was when he came back to see Harry and the rest of the family. Even then she couldn't be sure he would take the trouble to look her up. He cared about her deeply, she knew that from the way he spoke and the way he had once held her and kissed her, but would his feelings stay the same over long periods of absence? And wasn't she entirely to blame for the fact that he was keeping his distance?

She left him with his parents and went back to work. It was the best way she could think of to push the disturbing thoughts out of her mind.

Harry decided that he didn't want to miss out on a visit to his mother and so, as the weekend drew near, she tried to prepare for his stay at her cottage. She made up a bed for him in the guest room and made sure that everything was in place to welcome him.

On that particular Friday morning she was out on call with Theo once more. They were driving back to the hospital after treating a man who had suffered an accident at work when she asked him, 'What time do you have to leave for Somerset?'

He sent her a swift glance before turning his attention back to the road ahead. 'I'll go as soon as my shift ends. The charity event will be going on till late, so it won't matter if I'm not there right from the beginning. There will be plenty of time to talk with my ex-boss.'

'You said that he wanted to offer you a job,' she murmured. 'I suppose you'll be thinking it through. After all, your contract here comes to an end soon, doesn't it?'

He nodded. 'He wants to talk me through what's on offer. Apparently he's come up with something that has more scope than what I was doing before. It would allow me to widen my horizons and perhaps avoid some of the frustrating situations that I came up against before.'

'So you're giving it serious consideration?'

He sent her a thoughtful glance. 'I have to. It would give me a much more extensive role than I had under my previous terms of contract, and I need to talk through some of the issues.'

Megan was silent for a moment, absorbing the news. It was what she had predicted, and while she was happy for him that his future was expanding, the knowledge that he might leave for good made her more despondent than ever.

She was aware of Theo's gaze moving briefly over her. What was he thinking? Was he waiting for her to wish him well?

There was no time for her to say any more to him, though, because a call came out over the car phone just then, diverting them to a building nearby, where a teenager had been involved in a stabbing incident.

'It sounds pretty bad,' Theo commented as he turned the car in the direction of the shop premises where the assault had taken place.

Megan nodded, preparing herself mentally for what they might find. The emergency call operator had reported that the young man had tried to stop a thief raiding the till and had been stabbed, bleeding profusely from a chest wound as the thief had made his escape.

Theo parked the car and they raced into the corner store. The teenager was lying on the floor, and Megan could see straight away that he was in a dreadful state. He was gasping, thrashing about as his lifeblood ebbed away. He didn't look to be much more than around seventeen years old and as she watched him, her heart contracted painfully.

'How long has he been like this?' Theo asked the middle-aged storekeeper who kneeling over the boy, his face pale with anxiety.

'It must have happened ten minutes ago,' he said, moving back so that Theo could assess the patient. 'I didn't know what to do, and I wasn't sure how long it would take for the ambulance to get here, so I tried to stop the bleeding with a towel. It doesn't seem to be working.'

They both knelt down beside the young man. 'I'll put an airway in and get him on oxygen,' Megan said after she and Theo had made a swift examination.

Theo nodded. He was swiftly applying leads to the boy's chest so that they could monitor his heart activity, and then he made sure that they had intravenous access so that they could give him medication and any fluids he might need.

Theo's expression was grim as he pulled on surgical gloves. 'He's losing too much blood and his pulse is failing. His circulation's closing down. I think the knife must have penetrated his heart, and he's bleeding out.' His tone became urgent. 'If we don't act quickly, we're going to lose him altogether.'

Megan tugged her own gloves into place, her eyes widening as she glanced at the monitor. She said tautly, 'He's gone into cardiac arrest.'

Theo started to reach for his medical bag. 'We don't have any choice but to open up his chest,' he said briefly. 'The ambulance isn't here yet, and even if it was, he wouldn't survive the journey to hospital.' He took out a bottle of fluid that he used to swiftly clean the chest area, along with a pair of surgical shears.

She pulled in a deep breath. 'OK. What do you want me to do?'

'Help me by opening up the incision with the rib spreaders once I've cut through the sternum. I need to be able to expose the heart so that I can see what's going on.'

He was already operating as he spoke, and Megan worked quickly and efficiently to clamp the tissues in place. She could see that a huge blood clot had formed in the chest cavity, and Theo swiftly began to remove it.

'There's the hole in the heart that's causing the trouble,' he said a moment later. 'Can you put your finger in there to block it?'

Megan was already reaching out to do that, inserting her gloved finger into the wound made by the knife. The heart immediately began to fill up with blood once more, and she glanced towards the monitor. 'We have a pulse.' Her breathing steadied a little and she looked at Theo, marvelling at his coolness under pressure.

He was sedating the patient, making sure that he was anaesthetised adequately, and when he had finished, just as his glance meshed with Megan's, they both heard the sound of an ambulance siren. The noise was quickly cut off, and just a minute or two later the paramedics raced into the store.

'We are so glad to see you,' Theo said with a relieved smile. 'We need to get this boy to hospital right away.' His mouth made a wry shape. 'It looks as though Dr Rees will be going along with you on the journey.'

With her finger still blocking the hole in the boy's heart, Megan could only agree. She gave him a wan smile. 'Will you phone ahead and tell the emergency unit to prepare a theatre for him?'

'I'll do that,' Theo said. 'I'll see you back at the hospital.'

The journey in the ambulance was a nerve-racking experience for Megan. The boy's heart was beating fairly rapidly and his blood pressure was low. With any luck they would be able to suture the wound in his heart in Resus before transferring him to the operating theatre. Then a specialist cardiothoracic surgeon would take over his treatment.

Theo met her, as he had promised, going with her into the resus room where a team was waiting to receive the patient.

'I imagine your arm must be aching,' he said with a smile when she was finally able to withdraw her hand from the patient to allow a surgeon to suture the wound in the teenager's heart.

'You're not wrong,' she said, her mouth twisting. She looked him over. 'I see you've managed to clean yourself up and find a change of clothes.' She hadn't noticed that he had disappeared for a while at some point in the proceedings. 'I think I'll go and do the same.'

He looked immaculate, perfectly dressed in smart casual trousers and crisp linen shirt, and she guessed he was getting ready for his journey to Somerset now that their shift was drawing to a close. Would he still be there when she had showered and changed?

The boy was in Theatre when she came back into the central area of A and E some half an hour later, but as she looked around, there was no sign of Theo. Disappointment washed over her.

'Is there any news of how the boy is doing?' she asked Sarah. 'Theo was marvellous with him, and if it wasn't for his swift actions he would have stood no chance at all. I'd hate to see the lad go downhill now.'

'Theo went to find out,' Sarah responded. 'The boy's

parents have come in, and he spoke to them first of all. Now he's gone up to Theatre to see what's happening.'

So she hadn't missed him after all. Megan's heart gave a warming flip-over. She would have the chance to say goodbye to him. Somehow that mattered intensely.

'Ah…there you are.' The door swished open and Theo walked towards them. 'He's doing all right so far. His condition is stable for the time being and they're going to transfer him to the intensive care unit as soon as the preparations have been completed.' He shook his head. 'I wish I didn't have to go away. I'd really like to know what kind of recovery he makes.'

'I'll phone you and let you know when there's any news,' Megan told him.

'Thanks. I'd appreciate that.' He said goodbye to Sarah and then turned to Megan. 'Will you walk with me to the car park? I need to tell you about the arrangements for Harry.'

'Of course.' They walked towards the side doors and left the department, heading out of the hospital through the shady, landscaped quadrangle that led towards the staff car park.

At this time of day it was quiet out there, and Megan lifted her face to the sun where it filtered through the branches of the trees. The only sounds to disturb the peace were the occasional chorus of birdsong and the fluttering of leaves wafted by the gentle breeze.

'You were going to talk to me about Harry,' she reminded him as he paused in the shade of an ancient oak.

'So I was.' He straightened, as though he was gathering his thoughts together, and added, 'He's at a friend's birthday party, so if you could collect him from there around six o'clock, that would be great. He was going to take some of his cars over there, and his action figures, so perhaps you could remind him to bring them with him to your house.'

'I'll do that. They should help to make him feel more at home.' She glanced at him. 'Don't worry about him. I'll do my best to make things go smoothly for him.'

Theo smiled. 'I know you will.' After a moment's hesitation he drew her into his embrace and bent his head so that his cheek lightly brushed hers. 'I just wish that I could have done the same for you.'

She leaned into him, wanting the contact to go on for ever, revelling in the fact that his arms were around her. His words disturbed her, though, and she looked up at him, sending him an enquiring look. 'What do you mean?'

'Nothing. Forget I said it.' He dropped a kiss softly on her full lips and she absorbed it as though she was a flower that needed rain. 'It was never going to be easy for us, was it? Too much has happened to you in the past, so that you will always have doubts. I would have liked to be able to sweep them away, but I can't. As you said, it doesn't work that way.'

She frowned, holding onto him, her fingers trailing over the hard expanse of his rib cage. He was going away, just for a little while, but it was symbolic of what was to come. How would she survive without him in her life?

'Goodbye, Megan,' he said, the words a muffled whisper as he claimed her mouth once more.

She kissed him fervently in return, and then, too soon, he broke away from her, his mind moving on to other things, a ragged sigh hovering on his lips as he turned away. 'I'll call you,' he said.

She watched him go. Her heart was heavy, and her footsteps were leaden when she finally started to head back towards the hospital. She didn't stay to see him drive away. It would have been too painful.

CHAPTER ELEVEN

'LOOK,' Harry said, 'we all get a goody bag to take home...and I won one of the pass-the-parcel presents. It's a whistle, see?'

Megan not only saw but she got to experience the shrill sound as Harry blew hard on the whistle to demonstrate. 'Well, that's really something, isn't it?' she said cheerfully as they walked towards her car. With any luck, he would tire of blowing it before too long. 'It sounds as though you had a wonderful time at the party.'

'I did. We went rollerblading, and then we came back to Timmy's house for tea. We had sandwiches and cake and biscuits and jelly and ice cream.' He paused for a moment, laying a hand on his tummy. 'I had a lot to eat. I think I feel a bit sick.'

'Hmm.' Megan studied him closely for a minute or two. 'Perhaps it would be a good idea if I drive slowly, then.' She smiled.

Harry nodded. 'Timmy's puppy was sick,' he said as he clambered into the car and strapped himself in. 'He ate some of the cakes that the children dropped, and then people were feeding him biscuits. He was racing round and round the lawn, chasing us when we played football, and then after a bit he went sort of quiet and threw up in the flower border. He's all right now, though.'

'I'm glad to hear it.' Megan glanced in her rear-view mirror to make sure that Harry was settled before she started the engine and set off for home.

'Here we are,' she said a short time later. 'This is my house. It's not nearly as big as your Uncle Theo's, but there's a nice garden out back where you can play if you want. I asked the little boy from next door if he might like to come round and get to know you, and he said he would. His mother thinks the two of you would get on well together, being the same age.'

'What's his name?'

'Sam. He has some cars that he likes playing with, so you could show him yours if you like.'

Harry nodded, walking up the path to the front door and looking around. 'This is a pretty house,' he decided. 'I like the flowers over the door. Uncle Theo has flowers over the door like that, but the flowers are different.'

'Come on in and I'll show you your room.' Megan carried his overnight bag up the stairs and laid it down on the bed in the guest room. 'What do you think? Will you be all right sleeping in here tonight?'

Harry looked around. 'That's my racing-car poster on the wall, isn't it? And I've got a duvet cover just like that one.' He waved a hand towards the duvet that was printed with a racetrack complete with sleek sports cars.

'They're both yours. Theo lent them to me. He said you might like to have them here.' It was one of the things that made her love Theo all the more, the way he put so much thought into the child's well-being.

Harry nodded. 'This is cool. I like it.' He sent her a beaming smile, and Megan gave a soft sigh of relief. At least the first hurdle was over and done with.

The last time she had stayed with him overnight he had

pushed her away and told her that she wasn't his mother. Perhaps time had helped to heal some of his wounds.

The doorbell rang, and Megan said, 'I expect that will be Sam. Shall we go down and let him in? You can take your toys outside, and show them to him.'

Harry followed her down the stairs, and when she opened the door, Sam was standing there, as predicted, with his mother.

'We saw that you were home,' her neighbour, Theresa, said, 'so I thought this might be a good time to bring him around and introduce them to one another.'

She stayed to talk to Megan for a few minutes while the boys went to explore the garden. Megan made coffee for them, and some time later, when both children seemed to be happy in one another's company, Theresa left to go and prepare supper for her family.

Megan did likewise, doing a few chores here and there while the casserole heated in the oven, and all the time her thoughts strayed to Theo and his meeting with his ex-boss.

Was he pleased about the work that was on offer? Had his boss managed to come up with a contract that would satisfy Theo's need to use up-to-the-minute techniques and set schemes in motion that would ensure more lives were saved?

It was more than likely that he had. People were desperate to bring Theo on board, and she could understand their reasons for that, which did not add to her hopes he might stay.

'It's time for supper,' she called out to Harry some time later. 'You should come in now and wash your hands.'

While he was doing that, she escorted Sam back to his house, with the promise that he and Harry could play together another time.

Harry was tired but happy when she took him up to bed an hour or so later. 'Are we going to see my mum tomorrow?'

he asked. 'She's getting better every day, you know, and she wants to come home.'

'I know she is, and, yes, of course we'll go and see her tomorrow. We'll go to the hospital around lunchtime. That way, if she needs any help with her food we can be there for her.'

Harry was fidgety with excitement when they set off for the stroke unit the next day, but he didn't appear to be at all fazed when he saw a tall man leaving his mother's room as they arrived.

'That's Jonathan,' he explained, looking up at Megan as a line indented her brow. He waved an acknowledgement towards the man, who smiled and waved a hand in return. 'He works with Mum sometimes. He looks at the designs she makes, and then he takes them away and gets them made up in his factory. Sometimes I get to wear some of the clothes. They look to see if they're all right on me, but if I don't like them they don't bother with them any more.'

'Oh, I see.' Megan frowned. 'Are there many that you don't like?' She could see that being a problem for Francie if it happened very often.

'Nah. My mum's clever at that sort of thing, and Jonathan likes what she does.' He wrinkled his nose. 'I think they're a bit sweet on each other.'

'Really?' She sent him a thoughtful look, wondering at the adult phrase he used.

He nodded. 'That's what Uncle Theo says, anyway. He collected all the designs together when my mum was poorly and gave them to Jonathan so he could have them made into clothes. Then Jonathan came here and showed them to Mum. I think she liked that.'

They went into Francie's room and Harry went over to the

chair where his mother was sitting and threw his arms around her. 'See, I brought Megan with me today because Uncle Theo had to go to Somerset. Are you feeling better today? Will they let you come home soon?'

Francie nodded and hugged him in return. She looked over at Megan. 'Thanks for looking after him,' she said in a halting voice.

'You're welcome.' Megan smiled at her. 'We saw your friend leaving just now. I hope he hasn't left because he knew we were due to arrive.'

'No. He's gone to get coffee.' Francie tucked back a strand of dark hair that had fallen across her cheek. She used her good arm to do that, but then she said to Harry, 'I've been trying to walk with a stick. Do you want to see how I'm doing?'

Harry's eyes widened. 'Yes. Can you really do that?'

Francie nodded, and sent a quick look in Megan's direction. 'I might need a little bit of help.'

'Of course. I'm right here if you need me.' She knew that Francie would prefer to do this on her own, but she would stand near by just in case there was a problem.

Slowly, Francie rose to her feet and straightened up. She grasped the walking stick that was propped up at the side of her chair and took a careful step forward, then another.

'You're doing it, Mum. You're doing it.' Harry whooped with joy, and Megan felt like following suit.

'That's wonderful, Francie,' she said. 'It's absolutely wonderful.'

Francie smiled, and after a few more steps gingerly turned around to go back to her seat. 'It felt good,' she said, cautiously sitting down once more.

'Theo is going to be so pleased,' Megan told her. 'Does he know how well you're doing?'

'I think so. He's been so good—coming to see me and making sure things were going all right. And all the time he had his own problems.' She was silent then, tired after her efforts, as though she needed a moment to recover.

'You must have been worried about him,' Megan guessed. 'He gave up his job and seemed to be turning his back on everything before you were taken ill.'

Francie shook her head. 'You've helped him so much to get through all that. We're very grateful to you for what you've done, my parents and I. But Theo always does the right thing in the end. Other people were worried, but I knew he would work it all out.' Her expression was calm and relaxed.

Perhaps there was a unique bond between brother and sister. Megan could see that Francie was composed and absolutely certain in her faith in her brother. It was something special to see and it made her stop and think for a while. Why was Francie so sure of him, so convinced that he wouldn't put a foot wrong?

Jonathan came back after a while with coffee for himself and Francie. He chatted with the two women while he helped Francie to manage her drink, making sure that her hand was clasped firmly around the cup's specially designed holder and staying by her side to watch over her until she had finished drinking.

Then he talked to Harry, teasing him about the football club he supported, and they had a tussle, which ended in Harry giggling.

'I can see that they get along well,' Megan observed, looking at Francie, and she smiled in return.

'They do. That's just as well because I'm hoping that they'll be seeing a lot more of each other after I leave here.'

Megan's eyes widened. 'Do I take it that there's good news to come?'

Francie's mouth made a wider curve. 'There is, but we need to talk to Harry about it before we say anything more.'

That sounded to Megan as though things were really looking up. 'I'm really pleased for you.'

Some half an hour later Megan and Harry prepared to leave. 'I'm glad you're coming home soon,' he said, winding his arms around his mother's neck and kissing her goodbye.

Francie stroked his hair and looked up at Megan. 'Thanks for bringing him,' she mouthed silently, and Megan nodded, her lips curving.

Francie kissed her son and said softly, 'Things are going to work out just fine. You'll see.'

Back at home, Harry was a little subdued, but he didn't appear to want to tell Megan what was troubling him, and she left him to play with Sam in the garden, hoping that he would work through whatever it was.

She phoned the hospital to find out how the teenager was getting on in Intensive Care, and then she phoned Theo to tell him the news.

'He's awake and responsive,' she told him. 'Of course he's weak after all that he's been through, but they say he's doing very well, all things considered. They'll keep him in Intensive Care for a while longer, and then transfer him to a ward when the time is right.'

'That's brilliant news,' Theo said. 'I'm really glad that you rang me to let me know.'

For her part, she was just thrilled to hear his voice. It enveloped her, filling her with warmth and a sense of belonging, but more than anything she wanted to be able to reach out and touch him.

'How's Harry?' he asked, and she said that she would bring

him to the phone so that they could talk. She went to the kitchen door and called to Harry.

'Francie showed us how she could walk,' she told Theo as she waited for the boy to come in. 'It was fantastic to see, and Harry was thrilled to bits.'

'I knew she was getting there. That's great news.'

She wondered how things were going in Somerset, whether he had made any headway with the business of the two properties, his sister's and his own, but he simply said that he was going to talk to an agent the following day.

The thing uppermost on her mind was how the talks with his boss had gone, but his reaction to her question was similarly low key. 'I'm seeing him again later today so that we can talk some more.'

Harry ran into the kitchen then, and she handed the phone to him so that the two of them could talk. She busied herself with wiping down the surfaces, longing to have the chance to hear Theo's voice once more, but then Harry was saying goodbye to him and in the next instant he cut the call.

'Has he gone?' she said, and Harry nodded.

'I said 'bye,' he told her. 'Is it all right if I go back out to play now?'

'Yes, of course.' Theo would ring back if he wanted to talk to her. Only the phone stayed silent, and she tried not to let that bother her. He would be home tomorrow, wouldn't he? She had already spoken to him, so why was she hankering to hear his voice once more?

At bedtime, Harry's solemn mood returned. He was dressed in his pyjamas, and she watched him climb into bed, his movements slow and laborious, as though his thoughts were weighing him down.

She settled the duvet into place around him and sat down

on the side of the bed. 'Are you all right?' she asked. 'Is something troubling you?'

His mouth turned down at the corners. 'I don't want to go back to Somerset,' he said, after a while.

'You won't be going there, will you? Your mother will be going to your Uncle Theo's house, won't she? That's why Theo has had all the handrails installed.'

'Yes, but when she's better we won't be staying there, will we? And Uncle Theo is going back to Somerset. That's why he's gone to make sure the house is all right. I don't want him to go. I like him being here, and I like being near my gran and grandad, and all my friends are at my school.'

He reached out to her then, wrapping his arms around her for comfort and snuggling his head against her chest. Megan was overwhelmed by the simple, natural gesture, and held him close, a surge of tender emotion sweeping through her. This surely must mean that he had finally accepted her. It was a wonderful feeling.

'I don't think you need to worry about any of that,' she told him. She stroked his silky hair, drawing him to her and lightly kissing his forehead. 'Didn't your mother say that things were going to work out just fine?'

Slowly, cautiously, he nodded.

'Well, your mother wouldn't have said that if things were going to be different, would she? Besides, when I was talking to Jonathan, he said that he would be setting up another factory in Wales, so I think that must mean that your mother plans to stay here.'

'Does it?' Harry was frowning.

'I think so. I hope so. I have the feeling that your mother doesn't want to be far away from your gran and grandad.'

He gave her a hug and then lay down, resting his head against his pillow. 'Mum will need to use the handrails for a long time, won't she? So she'll want to stay at Uncle Theo's house.'

'I'm sure she will.'

He seemed to be content with that for the time being, and after a while his eyes began to droop with weariness. Megan waited until his breathing became long and even, and then she dropped a kiss on to his forehead before quietly leaving the room.

She wished that Theo was back here now, to soothe Harry's troubled mind and at the same time help to quieten her own uneasy thoughts. Like Harry, she didn't want him to go away. She wanted him close by, and there was an intense pain inside her at the thought that he would eventually be leaving. She had never loved anyone in the way that she loved Theo, and only he would know how to make things right.

She went into the living room and started to pace the floor. Wasn't there something she could do to resolve her own disquiet? Didn't the solution to her problems lie in her own hands? Theo had told her as much several weeks ago, but she had resisted doing anything about it, worried about stirring up past troubles.

Theo was right, though, wasn't he? How could she move on while there were issues that still needed to be faced? She couldn't do anything about the split with her mother…that was over and done with and she knew where she stood on that score. She had even managed to accept that her mother was a shallow creature who thought of herself first and foremost… But what about her father? Wasn't it time that she made a serious effort to talk things through with him, once and for all? Why shouldn't she do that, right here and now?

She went over to the phone, anxious to put her thoughts

into action before she had time to change her mind. For a moment or two she hesitated, but then she picked up the receiver and dialled his number, half afraid that he wouldn't be at home at this time of the evening.

The ringing tone stopped, though, and her father's voice came down the line, as clear as crystal.

'Megan, is it you? How are you? Is everything all right?'

'Yes, it's me, Dad. Everything's fine…I mean, I suddenly felt that I needed to call you, and just hear your voice.'

He must have detected a note of anxiety in her voice, because he said, 'You're upset about something, aren't you? Do you want to tell me about it? What's wrong?'

She wasn't sure what to say to him. 'It's nothing, really. I just…I suppose I needed to make sense of everything. I'm a bit mixed up…at a crossroads, if you like…and I'm not sure which way to turn.'

Her father was silent for a moment, perhaps waiting for her to say more, but when she didn't, he said quietly, 'This is about your mother, isn't it? What she did to you, to both of us, is something that has stayed with us throughout the years, and I don't know what I can do to put things right, Megan. I've thought about it, over and over again, and I wanted to do whatever I could to take away the pain and smooth things out for you. I just never managed to do that somehow.'

She shook her head. 'It wasn't your fault. It wasn't your mistake to put right.'

He gave a soft sigh. 'I don't know about that. I blamed myself for years for not being able to keep her with us. It hurt you so badly that I was angry—with your mother, with everyone and everything. I didn't realise that by thinking that way I was adding to your pain.'

'You couldn't help feeling the way you did.' All the angst

of the past years began to seep out of her. 'I was wrong to blame you. I wish I could make up for the way I treated you, for the way I poured all the troubles on your head. I knew it wasn't your fault, deep down. It was my mother's decision to go. She was the one who let us both down.'

'But I was the adult.' Her father paused for a moment, and she guessed he was thinking about that. 'You were just a child lashing out at the way your world had crumbled around you. I wanted so much to hold you and comfort you and tell you that everything would be all right, but I didn't know how to make that move. There was so much hurt. I couldn't make it better with a word or two. It went too deep for that.'

'You did what you could.' Megan gave a slight smile. 'You were always there for me through my school years, and it was you who encouraged me to go to medical school when I was worried that I might not be able to cope with it. You shored me up in a lot of ways that I didn't recognise at the time. It's only now that I'm beginning to look back on my life and see things differently.'

'I'm glad you've been able to do that.' Her father's voice became roughened with emotion. 'You know that I love you, Megan, don't you? I couldn't have asked for a better daughter. I've watched you working so hard to become a doctor, and I'm proud of what you've achieved. It worried me that your childhood might have blighted you for ever, but there comes a time when we have to put our fears behind us if we're ever to move on.'

'Yes,' she said softly. 'I've come to realise that, too. I've made the mistake of painting everyone with the same brush, and that was my downfall. It made me wary of everyone and everything.' She pulled in a ragged breath. 'I love you, Dad. I just wanted you to know that.'

'I'm glad you called me to tell me that, Megan.' Relief sounded in his voice, as though a weight had been lifted off him. 'It means a lot to me. You just need to know that I'm here for you, whenever you need me.'

'I know that, Dad.' She smiled again. 'I think I've always known that.'

She put down the phone a short time later and wandered about the room, thinking things through before she finally prepared for bed.

She spent a restless night, thinking over the conversation with her father, recalling the worries Harry had expressed about his home life and about Theo leaving for Somerset, and she wondered what might lie ahead for all of them.

After breakfast next day, she made jam tarts with Harry, so that by the end of the morning the kitchen was filled with the delicious smell of baking. She set the tarts out on wire racks to cool, and after tasting the fruits of his efforts, Harry went outside to explore the shrubbery.

Megan cleared away the baking utensils and was wiping down the kitchen worktops when she heard Theo's car pull up on the drive. She rinsed her hands and dried them on a tea towel, and then hurried to the front door to let him in.

'You're earlier than I expected,' she said with a smile, going into his arms as though he was her sustenance, the reason for her being. He kissed her briefly, thoroughly, as though he had missed her as much as she had missed him, and then stopped, lifting his head as if he would take stock of everything around him.

Perhaps her cramped hallway was not the best place to have a prolonged greeting. 'Come on in. Harry's in the garden.' She led the way into the kitchen, and he looked around, sniffing the air in appreciation.

'How did you know that I was hungry?' he asked, with a

mischievous smile. 'It was thoughtful of you to bake all these specially for me.'

She laughed. 'Help yourself, but leave some for Harry or there'll be trouble.'

He sank his teeth into the pastry and rolled his eyes as the flavour hit his tongue. 'Mmm…mmm…these are good. I'd never have gone away if I'd known you could produce food like this.'

'I made some tea,' she said, laughing at his banter and starting to pour the golden liquid into cups. 'How did it go? Did the talks with your ex-boss go in the way you expected?' She added milk and sugar.

'More or less,' he said. He sent her a cautious glance. 'He made me an offer that was very tempting.'

Under normal circumstances, that answer would have bothered her, but now she went to stand beside him, winding her arm around his waist. After thinking things through last night, she was much calmer now. 'But you didn't take it, did you?'

He looked at her curiously, a faint smile playing around his mouth. 'How do you know that?'

'Let's just say it was intuition.' She tilted her head to one side, looking up at him. 'I spoke to Francie yesterday, and something she said made me realise that I was worrying about nothing. I had to think about it for a long while, but then it all came home to me. Suddenly, I knew that you wouldn't take the job.'

'And how did you know that? What was it that she said to you?'

'She said you always do the right thing.'

He lifted a dark brow. 'Is that all?'

She nodded, and tugged at his shirt. 'It was enough. Stop teasing me and tell me that I'm right.'

'You could be right.' His mouth twisted. 'I persuaded my

former boss that the ambulance scheme we're running here was exactly the sort of scheme he should be running in Somerset, and he agreed to put it to the board. I suspect he'll be looking for new recruits to sign on for it some time in the near future.'

'But you won't be among them?'

He chuckled. 'I won't. In fact, John Edwards made me an offer I couldn't refuse. He's had talks with the trust board and he wants me to oversee the new emergency on-call doctor service that they'll be setting up. It's something I've come to feel very strongly about. Working with the ambulance service has helped to restore my faith in medicine. It not only gave me the impetus to get back to work, it made me realise that I've managed to conquer my demons, once and for all. I know I'm never going to feel the doubts that I had before. It's what I want to do. I'm there with the patient from the outset, and I know that by being there I have the best chance possible to save a life.'

She pulled in a shaky breath, overcome by the fantastic news. 'I'm so happy for you,' she said softly.

His fingers lightly threaded through her hair. 'You still haven't told me what made you so sure I wouldn't be going away.'

She snuggled close to him and rubbed her cheek against his chest, absorbing the warmth of him and feeling the steady beat of his heart run through her as though she was one with him.

'Francie meant that you make very careful decisions, and you always stand by your loved ones. They mean more to you than any offer of promotion, no matter how tempting, and you would never consider leaving her to fend for herself after all this time. You may have found someone to take care of her throughout the day when she comes home, but you would never leave her, or Harry. You started this, and you'll see it through until she's fully recovered.'

'I could still decide to leave at some time in the future.'

'But you won't.' She lifted her head and looked him in the eyes. 'It suddenly came to me what you meant when you said you wished you could make things go smoothly for me. You would have done anything to show me that you cared for me, loved me, even, but none of it would have been any good if I wasn't ready to accept that in my own mind.'

She ran her hand over his shirt, delighting in the feel of his hard, strong body. 'I had to know that you loved me and wouldn't leave me. It was something I had to learn for myself and believe in if we were to have any future together. Given my past, that wasn't an easy lesson, but I had a long talk with my father last night, and he helped me to see that I have to move on. I have to put the past behind me and learn to trust in people. You, Francie and Harry, and your parents have all shown me the way. You've drawn me into the fold. You're like family, and I know that none of you will ever let me down.'

'It feels so good to hear you say that. I'm glad that you found the courage to talk things through with your father.' He smiled into her eyes. 'I wanted you to understand how deeply I care for you, to know how certain I am that I would never leave you, but I wasn't sure that you would ever manage it.' He wrapped his arms around her and kissed her soundly for several minutes.

He drew in a shaky breath. 'So will you take that leap in the dark?'

She nodded, smiling up at him. 'As long as you're there with me.'

He bent his head and kissed her once more, his lips exploring the soft contours of her mouth, his arms drawing her ever closer to him.

The kitchen door rattled, and small footsteps sounded as a

faint breeze wafted through the room. 'Are you two kissing?' Harry said, pushing the door shut behind him. They drew apart slightly, both of them gazing down at him.

Theo's arms stayed around Megan. 'That's what we're doing,' he said. 'Is that OK with you?'

Harry's shoulders wriggled a little, and his face twisted a fraction as he thought about it. 'It's OK,' he said. 'Are you going to get married?'

Theo looked at Megan. 'I hope so,' he said. 'That's what people do when they love one another. What do you think about that idea?'

Megan's mouth softened. 'It sounds perfect to me,' she murmured. Her lips curved. 'Are you saying that you love me?'

'I do. For ever and ever,' he answered huskily.

Harry seemed to take that on board well enough. 'I thought you might,' he said. 'I saw the painting of Megan and I was pretty sure you would be getting married soon.'

Megan's eyes widened as her gaze swivelled to him. 'You were?'

He nodded. 'Uncle Theo told me he only paints special people. He's done ones of me and my mum, and Gran and Granddad cos he loves us, and you looked very pretty in your painting...all sunny and happy.'

Megan looked at Theo in wonder. 'Is that right?'

'Yes, that sounds about right to me. I wanted to capture your expression when you first sat there, as though life was blissful and you couldn't want for anything more. I think I managed to show that. I'm pleased with it at any rate. I just hope that you like it, too.'

He smiled down at her. 'I thought it might have pride of place in the home we'll share together.'

'Will it?' Her voice was breathless with all the joy that was flooding through her. 'And where will that be? You were talking about the house in Somerset...I'm not sure what you have in mind.'

'I don't know, exactly. That's something I thought we needed to talk about, but I guess it will be close to where I'm living at the moment. I don't know how you feel about us living at my house, because Francie will be staying there for as long as it takes for her to recover...or maybe even longer. I could sell the place in Somerset so that we can look around for a house of our own, if you like.'

'Couldn't we all stay in your house after we're married? I get along really well with Francie, and I love Harry to bits. To me, they're like the loving family I've been missing all these years, and I want to help take care of them. It would fill me with contentment to know that we belong together as a proper family. Later, when Francie has recovered completely, she can decide what she wants to do.'

He kissed her tenderly on the mouth. 'I hoped you might feel that way. Mind you, I think Jonathan will want to have some input on that score. He wouldn't be bringing a factory here to Wales if he didn't have some kind of a plan in mind. I'm pretty sure he and Francie will be tying the knot at some point.'

Megan lightly nuzzled his cheek. 'It all sounds...wonderful,' she said on a breathy sigh. 'You certainly seem to have thought everything through.'

Harry was still not clear about what exactly was going on. 'Does that mean you're not going away?' he asked. 'You're not going to live in Somerset?'

'I'm not,' Theo agreed. 'How can I possibly go away when you want a puppy to run around in the garden at home? Your mother won't be able to look after it for some time to come, so we'll have to sort out some solution where we can all take care of it until she's better, won't we? And that will have to be close by so that you can take it for walks with me and Megan.'

'Wow!' Harry said, jumping up and down. 'Do you mean it?'

Theo nodded.

Harry was beside himself with joy. 'A puppy...I'm going to have a puppy!'

He danced around the kitchen for a while and then stopped bouncing long enough to ask, 'Does my mum know about this? Has she said that it's all right?'

Theo nodded. 'Actually, it was her idea. She thought the walks would do her good once she's back on her feet properly. And Jonathan said he would come and see her every day and help out, too.'

'I'm going to have a puppy!' Harry was whooping again. 'I gotta go and tell Sam.' He rushed to the door, but then he paused and turned to say, 'I won't be long. I'll be back in a minute.'

'Take your time,' Theo said, his mouth curving as he lowered his head towards Megan once more. He drew her close to him. 'There's really no need for you to rush back.'

FREE

2 BOOKS AND A SURPRISE GIFT!

We would like to take this opportunity to thank you for reading this Mills & Boon® book by offering you the chance to take TWO more specially selected titles from the Medical™ series absolutely FREE! We're also making this offer to introduce you to the benefits of the Mills & Boon® Book Club™—

- ★ FREE home delivery
- ★ FREE gifts and competitions
- ★ FREE monthly Newsletter
- ★ Books available before they're in the shops
- ★ Exclusive Mills & Boon Book Club offers

Accepting these FREE books and gift places you under no obligation to buy; you may cancel at any time, even after receiving your free shipment. Simply complete your details below and return the entire page to the address below. You don't even need a stamp!

YES! Please send me 2 free Medical books and a surprise gift. I understand that unless you hear from me, I will receive 4 superb new titles every month for just £2.99 each, postage and packing free. I am under no obligation to purchase any books and may cancel my subscription at any time. The free books and gift will be mine to keep in any case.

M9ZEE

Ms/Mrs/Miss/Mr...Initials ....
BLOCK CAPITALS PLEASE

Surname ....

Address ....

....

....Postcode ....

Send this whole page to:
The Mills & Boon Book Club, FREEPOST CN81, Croydon, CR9 3WZ